# He admired Avery's strength of spirit and singleness of heart...

Avery didn't want this house for her own benefit, but to minister to others.

Jack realized that whether or not they built the resort here or within another small town, many of Avery's concerns were the same no matter where he went. He'd been smashing into small towns and changing them, for better or worse, since he'd started doing this job.

It gave him a lot to think about.

"I don't want to argue with you anymore," he admitted softly, reaching out and taking her hand.

She glanced down at where their hands met, but to his surprise, she didn't snatch hers away as he'd expected her to do. "Neither do I."

"Even if we're on opposite sides?" he asked in a whisper.

"Even then. Maybe especially then."

"Good." He hadn't expected it to be that easy for them to come to an understanding.

He captured her gaze...and saw the same astonishment registered there.

A *Publishers Weekly* bestselling and award-winning author of over forty novels, with almost two million books in print, **Deb Kastner** enjoys writing contemporary inspirational Western stories set in small communities. Deb lives in beautiful Colorado with her husband, miscreant mutts and curious kitties. She is blessed with three adult daughters and two grandchildren. Her favorite hobby is spoiling her grandchildren, but she also enjoys reading, watching movies, listening to music (The Texas Tenors are her favorite), singing in the church choir and exploring the Rocky Mountains on horseback.

Visit the Author Profile page at Harlequin.com for more titles.

# Opening Her Heart

## Deb Kastner

**LOVE INSPIRED**
INSPIRATIONAL ROMANCE

# LOVE INSPIRED®
## INSPIRATIONAL ROMANCE

Recycling programs
for this product may
not exist in your area.

ISBN-13: 978-1-335-55409-3

Opening Her Heart

This edition published by arrangement with Harlequin Books S.A.

For questions and comments about the quality of this book, please contact us at CustomerService@Harlequin.com.

Love Inspired
22 Adelaide St. West, 40th Floor
Toronto, Ontario M5H 4E3, Canada
www.Harlequin.com

Printed in U.S.A.

Jesus said unto her, I am the resurrection, and the life: he that believeth in me, though he were dead, yet shall he live: And whosoever liveth and believeth in me shall never die.
—*John* 11:25–26

To everyone who has lost someone
dear to them, and for those who are
caring for someone who is sick. I know there
are no words to make things better, but I pray
God's grace upon you all in a special way.
We don't know what tomorrow holds, so I pray
all of us will say "I love you" to the ones
we care for in our lives. We don't know—
but God does, and He's in control of it all.

# Chapter One

"Avery? Earth to Avery…"

Thirty-five-year-old Avery Winslow snapped out of her thoughts and turned her gaze to her best friend Lisa Gibbons, who was dangling a set of keys in her hand right in front of Avery's nose and grinning like the proverbial cat who'd eaten the canary.

Avery's heart welled until she thought it might burst clear out of her chest. She had been waiting absolutely forever for this moment, and now it was finally here. She wanted to pinch herself just to make sure it was real.

Technically, *forever* had actually only been a few months, but she was one of those people for whom, when she decided to do something, she wanted it done *now*. It was time to put those dreams into practice. Christmas had just passed, and she was finally able to look after her own interests instead of just her family's Christmas-tree farm.

"It's perfect," Avery murmured. "Don't you think it's perfect, Dandy?" she asked the black Lab mix at her heel. She always tried to take one of the service dogs in training from A New Leash on Love, her service dog ministry, with her whenever she went out, and today was no different.

Dandy sat and gestured with a paw.

"Good boy," she said, slipping him a bit of bacon for exhibiting the proper behavior. To Lisa she said, "See? Even Dandy approves."

Lisa grinned. "Did I tell you, or did I tell you? The moment I saw it, I knew you'd love it—and Dandy, too," she said with a laugh. "Gotta get his opinion in there, of course." She swept her arm toward the cabin in a big gesture that fit Lisa's gregarious personality, and what made her such a great real estate agent. "Talk about it being worth the wait! The cabin won't even be formally listed yet for another week, but I managed to speak to the owners and snag the keys so we can take a look inside," she said in a singsong voice.

"Get ready to be blown away. You aren't going to believe this."

"Was I impatient?"

"As if you have to ask," Lisa said with a snort. "You're pushy, too, by the way. It's a good thing you picked me to be your real estate agent and not someone else. They'd never understand your motivation the way I do. This is by far the biggest passion project I've ever seen you take on. You're usually too buried in the family businesses' financials to lift up your head and see the world. You think in spreadsheets."

"Just tell me what I need to know," Avery insisted, ignoring Lisa's jibes. They'd been best friends since kindergarten in Whispering Pines, Colorado, and even though they were now adults and Lisa had a family of her own, they still managed to get together for coffee at least once a month.

So, of course it made perfect sense to hire Lisa as her real estate agent when the timing was right for Avery to set her plans in motion.

As they approached the front door, Lisa supplied more information. "You already know the Meyer family from church. They built this cabin when their brood started growing, and they've lived here ever since."

While Avery was familiar with the Meyers, she'd never visited them at their home. She knew they had five children and were faithful Christians.

"The kids all grew up and moved away," Lisa continued, "and the place is obviously too big for just the aging couple. Six bedrooms and four baths, plus a separate mother-in-law suite. Tell me it's not perfect for what you have in mind. It couldn't get better than that if I'd planned it that way."

Avery examined the outside of the cabin. Tucked into the woods so it was nice and solitary, the peace surrounding the place was tangible. It was only a fifteen-minute drive to the center of town and ten to Winslow's Woodlands and the dog rescue, A New Leash on Love, which was the real key to the cabin's location.

"I adore the gorgeous wraparound porch." She was in love. And she was already making lists in her head—changes she wanted to make, tools and materials she'd need to purchase. Names of contractors to do the work for her.

Organize and Prioritize. That was her motto. "If I add a porch swing in that corner and some outdoor furniture, along with—"

She'd been about to share her thoughts about year-round landscaping and a vegetable garden, as well as a playground for visiting children, but at that moment, the roar of a car's engine overtook the sound of her voice.

*What on earth?*

Suddenly, a shiny red Mustang came around the curve of the driveway at a speed far too fast for the dirt road, and when the vehicle slammed to a stop, it fishtailed and nearly hit the side of Avery's blue SUV.

Avery gaped, but no sound came from her throat.

*Seriously?*

Who drove that way, especially on unpaved mountain roads?

"I thought you said the owners wouldn't be here this afternoon," she managed to squeak out.

"They aren't. I can assure you *that person* is not one of the owners," Lisa said, annoyance lining her tone. "As you well know, the Meyers are a lovely older couple who are moving to Arizona for retirement. And *that*—"

The man unfolded himself from the driver's seat and stood to his full over-six-foot height, let out a whoop of pure pleasure and waved his black cowboy hat in the air before combing his fingers back through his thick, dark hair and settling the hat on his head. He straightened it as if he were looking at his reflection in a mirror and wanted his image to be *just so*.

Lisa croaked something else out, but it was entirely inaudible.

Two things struck Avery simultaneously. First, the man who'd exited the vehicle was most definitely *not* even close to retirement age, and second, she'd never seen him before in her life.

It wasn't so much that they didn't have strangers occasionally visiting Whispering Pines. Avery's own family brought in customers from all over Colorado who wanted the full Christmas-tree-cutting experience or who sought to purchase specialized landscaping during the rest of the year. People needed evergreen bushes or aspen trees, and Winslow's Woodlands offered a little bit of everything. They were known for being the best.

So, yes, there were often strangers in town. But this man?

He was as out of place as a blue spruce in an orange grove. And he was on land *she* intended to purchase—before anyone else was supposed to know about it.

Yes, he sported a cowboy hat and boots similar to those that the men around the Pines wore, but his suit, complete with obsidian cuff links that he highlighted with an annoyingly obvious adjustment, was *way* over the top for a quiet mountain town. Their lawyers and judges didn't wear such obnoxiously expensive suits. The whole getup probably cost more than Avery made in a year, and his new boots gleamed from a fresh polish.

Avery fought to withhold a grin, thinking about how quickly those shiny boots would lose their luster with all the dirt he'd raised with his foolish driving.

Served him right.

Then the other thought immediately made the smile drop from her lips.

What was this stranger doing *here*?

"And didn't you say the cabin wasn't listed

yet?" Avery said quietly through a dry throat. She coughed to clear her voice. "What does this guy think he's doing here?"

"It hasn't been listed," Lisa whispered back. "I'm positive of that. I have no idea how—"

"Good afternoon, ladies," said the man as he tipped his hat, accompanied by a sparkle in his deep blue eyes and a grin Avery could only categorize as charismatic. Or maybe *obnoxious* was the better word for it. He could easily have starred in a toothpaste commercial.

She had a bad feeling about this—a *very* bad feeling.

As the man approached, the puppy at Avery's heels started barking and straining against his lead—something he'd been in training not to do. Was he trying to protect her, to tell her this man was bad news?

She wouldn't have been surprised if that was so. In her experience, dogs were good judges of character. But if that was the case, they lost the battle within moments, as the man quickly won over her dog, crouching before him and holding out his hand palm down so Dandy could sniff it and then scratching the dog behind the ears, earning him a happy welcome lick on his well-trimmed, bearded cheek.

The man chuckled. "You're a cute little puppy, now, aren't you?" the man murmured in the high pitch people typically used with animals and small children.

Avery felt frozen to the spot, which was unlike her. While she didn't exactly consider herself as a people person so much as a businesswoman, she knew how to handle herself. Yet, there was something about this man that threw her off. Fortunately, Lisa stepped into the gap, stepping forward and offering her hand. The man stood to his full height and enthusiastically returned her shake.

He was solidly built, with broad shoulders that pressed at the seams of his suit. Yet Avery didn't think it was his height that intimidated her. Rather, it was his presence.

"Lisa Gibbons of Gibbons Realty. And you are?"

"Super stoked to be here," he said in what could only be a genuine Texas drawl. That explained the cowboy hat and boots, anyway. "Not that I mind drivin', and the winter scenery around here could knock a man's socks off."

Avery didn't want to think about the man's socks, which were probably made of pure gold. And it didn't pass her notice that he hadn't answered Lisa's question.

"I'm Avery Winslow," she said, hoping the man would pick up the slack in the names department. "Of Winslow's Woodlands."

"Right. Jake Cutter, from Marston Enterprises."

A tight knot formed in the pit of Avery's stomach. She had no idea what Marston Enterprises was, but it sounded ominous. This couldn't be good, a stranger arriving in town representing some big-name company.

Why had this gregarious, ostentatious man shown up at *her* future bed-and-breakfast? It wasn't exactly right off the road. More like off the beaten path, which was the whole point of her choosing this place.

"What are you doing here?" she asked bluntly.

He held up both hands, palms out in a sign of surrender, and took a step backward. "Whoa there, Ms. Winslow," he said with another toothy grin. "No reason to get your dander up. What fun would it be if I gave away all my secrets right out of the chute?"

"It's Avery," she said automatically, then immediately regretted it, realizing she'd just eliminated the mental distance between them by putting them on a first-name basis.

"Call me Jake," he said, but he wasn't looking at her. Instead, his gaze was gliding over the house and onto the land around it.

"Nice-looking place you have here."

Avery didn't yet have it, but she would. Despite the stranger's unexplained appearance, excitement crept back up into Avery's heart.

"We were about to take a tour inside the cabin," Lisa said. "We'd be happy to have you accompany us."

Avery sent her best friend a glare and raised her eyebrows. What did Lisa think she was doing, inviting the guy in?

Lisa shrugged and gestured to her clipboard. Avery supposed she couldn't blame her for trying to get new business, especially since the man had shown up without a real estate agent. She was probably thinking about nabbing the guy as a client.

A very rich client.

But not in connection with *her* future bed-

and-breakfast, thank you very much. Lisa knew she wanted this place. There was no way she'd betray her in this. She would have to point this Jake fellow in a different direction, which was, now that Avery thought about it, probably what Lisa intended to do.

As it was, Avery was much more inclined to tell Jake Cutter to get back into his fancy red Mustang and see himself off the property—without taking a tour of the house and land.

She usually didn't mind a little competition in her life. With five brothers and sisters, she'd grown up with a competitive spirit.

Just not now. Not for this. It was too important to her, and the sooner they wrapped up the particulars, the better.

Apparently, however, this place meant something specific to Jake, as well, though she couldn't begin to guess what it was he wanted with the place.

Jake grinned and tipped his hat a second time. "I appreciate the offer—Lisa, was it? But I don't need to see the inside of the cabin. I'm here for the land."

Jake chuckled as he watched the women make their way into the cabin. That Avery

Winslow was a beautiful spitfire, tall for a woman, with sparkling blue eyes and her blonde hair pulled back into a ponytail. He'd have to watch out for her.

It was more what she hadn't said than what she had. He hadn't gotten where he was in life today by accident. He had a gift with people. He'd made a study of reading expressions and body language and could practically guess what people thought before they'd figured it out themselves.

And it was clear that Avery Winslow didn't like him.

Which really should be neither here nor there—unless she ended up being the president of the town council, in which case it could be a very big problem indeed. He needed certain people in this town to be on board with his plans—or rather, Marston Enterprises' plans—but Avery more than likely wasn't one of them.

He didn't know why Avery's clear rejection bothered him, exactly. In the business he was in, renovating old land and buildings to become upscale resorts, it wasn't about making friends. He never stayed in any one place long enough to form any real relationships, which was just as well as he didn't care to make any. He'd pop into town for a few weeks to make the necessary connections, then move on to his next conquest.

That said, most people fell for his natural charm. It was part of what made him so successful. Getting to know people was easy, as simple as switching on his smile. Which was why Avery's immediate dislike of him set him on edge, he supposed.

He spent the better part of ten minutes walking around the land and surveying the area. He had studied a land map before he'd come, and the company had already decided this was the spot for a grand hotel. It was twenty minutes away from a major ski slope but secluded enough to draw in the type of clientele who Marston Enterprises wanted to attract.

Actors, sports icons and other celebrities would be visiting this place when it opened. Once the papers were signed, it wouldn't take long for them to build. He was just checking out the property for himself before he got down to the real business of getting the town council to vote the building permits and zoning in his favor.

He didn't need to see the inside the cabin, which was quaint in its own way but had definitely seen better days, because it would just be leveled in order for the new construction to go up.

Still, his encounter with Avery had made him curious—and it felt more than a little bit like a challenge. He never walked away from a challenge—especially such a pretty one.

He let himself into the cabin, whistling as he casually sauntered into the house.

"Hello?" he called, wondering where the women had gotten to. "Anyone home? Where'd y'all get to, now, anyway?"

He wandered through the front room and poked his head into a large, empty room he assumed was supposed to be the dining room. He then walked into an oversize kitchen with an industrial-size refrigerator and oven that took his breath away. In the middle was a gorgeous solid-oak island with a marble inset on it for food prep.

His mind drifted for a moment as he pictured himself and Lottie sitting next to each other on the stools at the island. He'd be serving his daughter the monkey-shaped chocolate-chip pancakes she especially loved.

Too bad the whole cabin would be torn down soon. He blinked hard to erase the daydream from his mind.

"Excuse me?" came a feminine but definitely annoyed voice from behind him. The deep, rich alto vibrated across his skin.

Ah—Avery had found him at last.

He turned and grinned, sweeping his hat off his head. He'd get it right this time—just to prove to himself he hadn't lost his ability to charm the ladies.

"I thought you said you didn't need to see the inside of the cabin." Again, Avery's bluntness surprised him. No beating around the bush with this woman. She laid it out plain and clear.

"I didn't. I don't." It wasn't like him to stammer, and he swallowed hard against the dry tickle in his throat. "I was just curious, so I let myself in. Lisa here said I could visit if I wanted, right?"

He was more curious about Avery than about the inside of the cabin, if truth be told, but he knew saying *that* thought aloud would get him into a world of trouble and hurt, so he just tapped his hat against his thigh and waited for her response.

"If you give me your cell number, we can set up a time to meet in regard to your needs," the real estate agent said, holding her clipboard toward him. "I'm sure I will be able to provide you with several wonderful choices in land around here. If I don't already know of something, I'll work to find a property that will be perfect for your company's needs."

"That won't be necessary," he assured her, ignoring the clipboard and instead shoving his hands into the front pockets of his slacks. "I've already done my homework, as has my company. If they haven't already, Marston will soon start the official paperwork to secure the property."

Avery and Lisa passed glances Jake couldn't even begin to decipher.

"I'm sorry. I don't understand. Because right now, all I know is you shouldn't be here," said Avery.

More like she didn't *want* him to be here, but he didn't correct her.

"Again, I just want to remind you I was invited inside," he said, nodding toward Lisa. "I thought I'd take a look around the place. Out of curiosity, I mean. Not because I need to know."

Avery remained silent.

"And while we're on the subject, why are *you* looking at the property, if I may ask?" he said, turning the tables on her.

"Not that it's any of your business, but I intend to remodel this beautiful cabin into a bed-and-breakfast for the customers of my family's businesses, especially because they often need to stick around for a couple of weeks to do the necessary training to receive a service dog to suit their needs. Many of them are facing major difficulties in their families as it is, and my vision is for them to have a quiet, peaceful place to stay."

"Bed-and-breakfast, huh?" He thoughtfully brushed a palm across his well-trimmed beard. It was a nice enough cabin, and the large kitchen was spectacular, but it was pretty run-down and would take a lot of elbow grease to get it into any kind of shape to serve customers. It'd be much easier just to raze the thing.

Besides, his idea for new construction was much, much better than a quiet bed-and-breakfast. And who knew? Maybe some of Avery Winslow's customers would enjoy a stay at the new resort—at least, the ones with deep pockets.

"The kitchen is outstanding, I'll give you that," he said, gesturing his head toward the kitchen doorway. "I'd really enjoy giving that oven a whirl."

"You *cook*?" she asked, her mouth agape as she looked him up and down.

He squared his shoulders. Why he felt offended by her response was beyond him. As if it mattered one way or another what she thought. "You don't have to sound so surprised. I spent a few really good months going to culinary school before I started working as a salesman. Ask my daughter, Lottie, if you don't believe me. I make a mean chocolate-chip pancake in any shape you want. Monkeys are Lottie's favorite."

"It's j-just that—" she stammered and then broke off. "I guess your fancy suit kind of threw me for a loop there."

He glanced down at his clothing and shrugged. "Marston has a dress code. And as a salesman, I try to look my best. I'm way more casual in the kitchen. Jeans and T-shirts on the weekends."

"Right."

He laughed. "You still look confused."

"I am. You never answered my question. What exactly does Marston Enterprises want with this cabin? What exactly is it that you do?"

"It's not the cabin we want, it's the land. We build upscale resorts, and this area is perfect. It's close to the ski slopes and only an hour and a half from Denver International Airport. There is a major highway nearby, but Whispering Pines is a nice small town tucked into the mountains.

"This town could be the new Aspen. Doesn't it excite you just a little bit that you might be having famous movie stars and sports icons wandering around Whispering Pines? Brand new businesses will move into the area to attract the types of customers our resorts bring in."

Her mouth grew wider with every word of his explanation. Clearly she wasn't nearly as happy about the possibilities as he was, which cut him to the quick. He apparently wasn't doing a very good job selling the idea to her.

"You don't really mean to—"

"I do. Well, Marston Enterprises does. The process is already in motion, so it's a little late to put the brakes on it now. Plans have been made, meetings convened."

"But this is *my…*" Her lips curled into a frown and lightning shot across her face. "What did you say will happen to my cabin?"

"I'm afraid it'll be torn down to make way for a grand hotel. Sorry." He shrugged. He really was sorry, since the place clearly meant so much to Avery.

"If you think you can just waltz in here and change the dynamics of our beautiful little town without getting any pushback, you have another thing coming."

Again, he shrugged. "I've done it before, and I'll do it again. And for the record, I'm good at what I do. I rarely receive any pushback from local town councils. Do an internet search on Marston Enterprises, and you'll see just how successful we are in this type of endeavor."

"I assure you I'll be doing that," she said.

"Good. Then you'll have the opportunity to see how truly beautiful these resorts are. It's totally worth whatever small inconveniences you have to give up. There's a good reason the rich and famous seek out Marston properties when they want to take time off. And it's not necessarily a bad thing for the town, either, you know," he said, his throat closing around his voice. He cleared his throat and evened out his tone. "Just the opposite, in fact. Think of all the money the resort will bring into this quaint little town."

"It won't be a *quaint* little town if you build your resort here," she pointed out wryly, her blond eyebrows forming a V over her nose.

"At the very least, shopping will boom," he insisted. "What exactly is Winslow's Woodlands?" he asked, thinking he might be able to use her own business as a case in point and turn the tables on her. She was thinking of making the cabin into a bed-and-breakfast, after all, which smacked of some kind of tourism. Maybe his customers could be hers, as well.

"It's a Christmas-tree farm. During the Christmas season we sell evergreens—offering either precut or the pick-and-cut-your-own experience. The rest of the year, we provide for customers' regular landscaping needs. Bushes and aspen trees, along with annuals, perennials and various types of rocks. You think your movie stars are going to want to go rock shopping while they're here?"

Her sarcasm wasn't lost on him.

"So, I'll admit," he said, "our resort may not directly affect your business, although some of our clientele may want to grab a dozen roses for their special someone."

"I didn't say we're a flower shop. We don't do roses."

"Okay, so maybe not, then. But you have to admit, many other businesses will get a big boost from serving our wealthy guests."

Avery seemed to be biting her tongue or clenching her jaw—or maybe both. And Jake felt as if he was digging himself deeper and deeper into a hole with every word he spoke, which was an unusual feeling for him. He was usually so slick with his words. But something about Avery pushed him off-balance.

Maybe because he'd seen in the flicker of her gaze just how much she cared about this place, although he couldn't imagine why.

A cabin was a cabin was a cabin. She could easily find somewhere else equally as serviceable as this one, probably even better. As he'd noticed when he'd first entered, this place would take a lot of work to bring it up to par for any kind of guest.

"They also have a service-dog program," Lisa offered, tapping her pen against her clipboard. "I think those clients were the guests to whom Avery was referring."

"Right. You said something about that earlier. And of course you've got this dog with you," he said, gesturing toward the dog, who was lying at Avery's heel. "You mean you train dogs for blind people?"

Avery snorted. It made Jake want to chuckle, though he knew that would probably just get him into even more trouble than he already was, so he kept his amusement to himself.

"Yes, like dogs for blind people," Avery snapped. "And for many other situations, as well."

"So what's this little guy here for?" he asked, reaching down to the black Lab and scratching behind his ears.

"This is Dandy. He's in training, so he needs to get out and experience different environments, including this one. We're watching him to see where he shows potential. But see, what you're not getting here is this place, this exact cabin, is the perfect location for those clients who come in to train with their new service dogs. They are usually under a lot of stress and need the peace that comes along with the seclusion and scenery this property provides. That's why it has to be this specific cabin and not somewhere else. Trust me, I've been looking for a long time, and I know I won't find anything better that's close enough to work for our clients. You, on the other hand—"

"Can't do anything to change what's about to happen. Marston probably already has their lawyers drawing up papers, and if they don't, they will soon. They've made their decision, Avery. I'm really sorry. This is the property they've chosen, and that's all there is to it."

"If it's a done deal, then what are you even doing here?" she asked, her words as sharp as a sword. "And why don't the Meyers seem to know anything about this?"

"I've come to Whispering Pines to settle things with the town council. Grease the wheels. Take care of permits and zoning issues as they arise. Obviously, Marston wants to make the transition as easy as possible for everyone involved."

"Obviously." Sarcasm dripped from her

tone. "It must be nice to be able to see so well from that high horse of yours."

"I'm trying to help," he insisted. It wasn't the first time he'd come up against resistance in a small town. To some degree, it was to be expected. No one really liked change. There was always someone digging in their heels against progress.

But Avery—well, she was making this personal, about herself and her bed-and-breakfast.

"I'm here to answer questions and make the whole process as painless as possible for everyone concerned."

Her eyes widened. "Painless? Yeah. Good luck with that. Come on, Lisa. Show me the mother-in-law suite you were telling me about. I'm sure it will be perfect for the managers of my new bed-and-breakfast."

# Chapter Two

It had been three days, and Avery still felt steam coming out of her ears every time she thought about Jake Cutter, with his perfect smile and fancy suit. It was now Sunday morning, and she ought to be focusing on preparing to worship the Lord at Whispering Pines Community Church, but try as she might, the annoyingly handsome man's face kept popping into her mind and making her nerves crackle.

She didn't know why the whole thing bothered her so much. Lisa was her real estate agent, and she had a personal relationship with the Meyers. Friends and neighbors stuck together around here. Surely they would win this little competition based on that alone.

There was something to be said about small-town connections.

Except Jake represented a large corporation and no doubt had piles of cash and a horde of lawyers behind him. He'd been forthright enough to admit he was here to convince the town council it was in Whispering Pines' benefit to zone the area for a resort such as Marston intended to build.

*It could happen.*

Maybe she should just walk away from it all before she got too invested and got burned.

*Probably* she should.

She didn't have the time or the inclination to tussle with the big leagues. If she waited long enough, Lisa would be able to find her other properties. She'd eventually be able to settle on something she could make work, even if it took more time and reconstruction. But the thought made her heart sink.

She didn't want to settle.

Because the moment she'd seen the Meyers' cabin, she'd known it was the one—the one which she'd been making scrapbooks about since their service-dog business had taken off and the need had presented itself. The one for which she still poured over home-design magazines, looking for new ideas for every room of her perfect bed-and-breakfast.

She would heartily agree with Jake that the beauty of the surroundings was worthy of a high-class resort. The problem was he didn't see any worth at all in the quaint cabin itself. He—or rather, his company—would raze it to the ground without a second's thought.

But for Avery, she couldn't ask for more in a home meant for a bed-and-breakfast for her special clients. The wraparound porch, the industrial-size kitchen, the large, open-space living room for guests to enjoy a spectacular view out of the window wall. It even had that private mother-in-law suite for whomever ended up managing the property.

*Perfect.*

Granted, it would take a lot of effort and elbow grease to get it ready for customers, but wasn't that half the fun? Scrubbing, painting, putting in new flooring and hanging up homemade curtains.

Her younger sister Ruby popped her head into Avery's bedroom. "Are you about ready to leave? If we don't hurry, we won't get our seats."

Avery chuckled. That wasn't exactly true.

The Winslows had taken up the third-and fourth-row pews on the left-hand side for as long as Avery could remember going to church. Some things had changed—she and her siblings had all grown to adulthood, her parents and her grandmother had passed on, and Logan Maddox and his son, Judah, had joined the family when Logan had married Molly—but everyone in the town knew they always sat in the same spot for every service. Even if an occasion ever cropped up where they'd be late, which there never had been, their places would be saved.

"Who are you taking?" Ruby asked as she placed a service-dog harness on a border-collie mix named Bandit. All the Winslow girls tried to take a dog to church—and everywhere else they went. It was important that the canines learn to remain calm and quiet in all situations, and church was especially good practice.

"I've got Tugger," she said, speaking of the sweetest brown-and-white pit bull mix the world had ever known. "He's already in the van. Felicity is taking Roxie." Roxie was unusual in that she was a purebred standard poodle given to them by an elderly neighbor who could no longer take care of her. She was a couple of years older than most of the pups but was whip smart and at the top of the canine class.

Even with the chaos of dogs in the van, they arrived at church well before the steeple bell rang, even with her brother Frost driving. He and Sharpe generally took turns at the wheel, but Avery preferred Frost's more predictable pace to Sharpe's more daring speed.

With their brothers alongside to help, the sisters situated themselves with their dogs and entered the church. Avery's eyes immediately scanned the room for Jake but didn't see him and let out the breath she hadn't realized she'd been holding.

It was no surprise, really. He didn't live in town, and she had no idea if he was a Christian or not, so there was no reason to expect him.

"Are you looking for someone?" Ruby asked curiously, scanning the room as Avery had just done.

"What? No, no one special," Avery answered. She wasn't ready to share her encounter with Jake Cutter, not even to her siblings. She just couldn't talk about it without getting *sangry*—a big ball of sad and angry.

She wasn't certain she wouldn't explode, when just thinking about him nearly set her off.

She did see a tall, regal-looking, gray-haired woman she didn't recognize standing close to the door of the sanctuary, holding the hand of a darling, dark-haired little girl Avery guessed to be about three years old.

Always happy to greet newcomers to the church, she approached the woman and smiled. The little girl beamed when she saw Tugger.

"Hi. I'm Avery Winslow. Are you new to Whispering Pines or just visiting?" she asked.

"My name's Elaine," she said. Her voice was naturally soft and held the soft hint of an accent. "And yes. We just arrived in town this week. We won't be permanent residents, but we'll be here for an extended period of time. We've settled in at one of those pretty little cottages along the creek."

"It's lovely over there. And what's your name?" she asked the little girl, who only had eyes for the dog.

"Lottie," she exclaimed.

Tugger did amazingly well with the outburst and didn't budge an inch. He just cocked his head and stared at her with interest, giving her a big smile. Avery slipped him a tiny bit of bacon and whispered, "Good boy.

"This is Tugger," she said. "And guess what? He loves little girls better than anyone else. Is it okay if Lottie pets him?" she asked Elaine. "Tugger is the sweetest, gentlest dog you'll ever meet."

Lottie looked up at the woman Avery assumed was her mother. "Can I pet Tugger, Grandma?"

That surprised Avery. Elaine hardly looked old enough to be a grandmother.

"Of course, sweetheart. Remember to be gentle when you pet him, though."

"I don't know if maybe I'm losing my mind or what's going on here, but I am positive that is not the dog I saw you with the other day," said an affable, Texas-accented male voice from right behind Avery's shoulder.

She stiffened, and her fists clenched of their own accord.

*Jake Cutter.*

Jake watched Avery's shoulders become rigid as he joined their little group. Apparently, she hadn't gotten any closer to getting over him swiping the land right out from underneath her. He supposed he couldn't blame her for that. It had come as quite a shock to her. One minute she was house shopping, and the next it was taken away from her.

"What's this one's name?" he asked, reaching down to give the dog a scratch behind his ears.

"Tugger," Lottie answered, enthusiastically throwing her arms around the dog's neck. "Can we please have a dog, Daddy?"

"Aw, Lottie, you know we've talked about this before." At least a couple of dozen times this year. She'd asked over and over for a dog. Not a pet—a dog. They were her favorite animals, after monkeys. He hated not being able to give Lottie exactly what she wanted in life, but a dog was out of the question, because of all the traveling they did.

Lottie pulled away from Tugger, so Jake scooped her up into his arms and gave her a noisy kiss on her cheek.

"I see you've met my mom and daughter," he said to Avery.

"I— Well, yes, I did."

He could see the confusion in her eyes and

realized she must not have known to whom she was speaking before he'd come up behind her and surprised her. He'd dropped his mom and Lottie out front of the church and had gone to find a place to park. When he'd entered the building, his gaze had instantly landed on Avery, and he'd made a beeline for her, anxious to see if she'd made peace with the situation between them.

Obviously not, but that only meant he had to work harder to win her over. He'd never before walked away from a challenge, and he wasn't about to start now. That Avery was especially attractive only made the idea of winning her over even that much sweeter in the end.

He should probably be working the room to discover whose attention he should be focusing on in this small town, but he'd have plenty of time to do that after the service was over. Right now, all of his concentration was on the pretty woman standing next to him.

"My mom and I always try to visit the local church every Sunday when we're new in town. This is a beautiful little church. Have you been going here long?" he asked, trying to keep things cordial between them, if not outright friendly.

"I was born and raised in Whispering Pines and was christened here when I was just a newborn, the same as my brothers and sisters."

"Brothers and sisters? Do you have a large family?"

Despite the look in her eyes that said she wanted nothing whatsoever to do with him, she chuckled. "You could say that. I have my grandfather, three sisters and two brothers—I'm the oldest, followed by my brother Sharpe, my sisters Molly and Ruby, then my brother Frost and last is Felicity. I also have a brother-in-law and a nephew. We take up two whole pews in church."

He laughed. "I'd love to meet everyone. Do y'all work together in the family businesses?"

Her brow lowered. She was staring at him as if he was trying to uncover some secret information that would work against her on his business deal, which was the furthest thing from the truth.

Actually, he was just trying to spark a conversation.

"We do. We're all involved to some extent in both the tree farm and the service-dog program, although it varies from sibling to sibling."

"What do you do? Train the service dogs, I take it, since you've had a dog with you both times I've seen you?"

"No, not really."

She'd caught him off guard with her answer, and it took him a moment to recover. "I'm sorry. I just assumed—" He gestured toward Tugger. "I mean, I've seen you with two different dogs now. It only makes sense that you were putting your effort into dog training."

"It takes a lot of time and energy for a dog to learn to be a service dog. They have to experience many different environments so they can learn to remain calm and focused, no matter where they are. My sisters and I take different dogs around with us virtually everywhere we go—to the store, restaurants—"

"Church," he finished for her.

"Yes," Avery agreed with a nod. "Including church. If you want to know who my sisters Ruby and Felicity are, just look for the dogs."

Jake would have said more, but the bell in

the steeple rang, and the people around them started moving toward the sanctuary.

"Would it be possible to bring Lottie over to see what you do sometime?" Elaine asked. "I'm sure she'd love to meet all of your dogs, and your program sounds fascinating, something I'd really be interested in learning more about. Or is that something you keep private?"

"Mom," Jake said, combing his fingers back through his hair, "I'm sure Avery doesn't have time to—"

Avery cut him off. "I'd love that. I'm sure Lottie would like to meet all our dogs. We also have a petting zoo with all kinds of animals, including a couple of really friendly donkeys and some goats and sheep and alpacas. What do you think about that, Lottie?"

"Yes, please," the little girl said politely. Jake's heart filled with such warmth, he thought it might burst.

How could he say no to that?

"I guess we'll be visiting Winslow's Woodlands, then," he said with a grin.

"And A New Leash on Love. That's what the service-dog rescue is called."

"Right, then." He pulled a platinum business card holder out of his pocket and handed her one of his cards. "This has my cell phone number on it. Call me when you have the chance, and we can set up a time to stop by."

For a long moment, she stared at the card as if she'd catch cooties, but she finally reached out and took it.

"Okay. Will do," she said at last. "Elaine, it was very nice meeting you. And it was especially nice meeting you, Lottie."

Jake's gaze followed Avery as she walked away, joining a few other adults he assumed were probably her siblings. He noticed she hadn't said anything about it being nice to see him again, not that he would expect her to.

Elaine followed the path of Jake's gaze and chuckled. "She is certainly a lovely young woman."

Only half listening, he nodded, but when he glanced down at his mother, he realized there was a mischievous quality to her tone and a sparkle in her gaze.

"No, Mom." He shook his head emphatically. "I mean, yes, she's attractive, and I'm sure she's a very nice person, but she's not for me."

His mother knew why he was not now, and

would not in the future, be looking to fall in love. He'd had a wonderful marriage with Lottie's mother, Amber, and the guilt he carried from the horrible way she'd died still burdened him tremendously. There wasn't a day that went by that he didn't think about Amber.

And his current predicament with Avery Winslow was the absolute furthest thing from romance.

No. This was 100 percent business, and nothing more.

Except, perhaps, a visit to a petting zoo.

# Chapter Three

Avery sipped at her coffee and watched as Jake worked the fellowship hall. He fit in a little better today, wearing a casual sport coat and slacks, though she was certain his clothing was of much finer quality than anything her friends and neighbors could afford. Everything was clearly tailored to fit his tall, muscular build, and the look worked for him.

She might not like him, but even so, she had to admit he was quite an attractive man.

He hadn't waited five minutes after the church service was over before he'd headed straight for the fellowship hall, his smile in place and motivation shining from his eyes. He was a man with a purpose. Too bad she couldn't make a public announcement to warn her friends and neighbors that he had an ulterior motive for being here. He was giving the word *fellowship* a brand-new meaning.

As far as she could tell, he wasn't approaching anyone specifically—at least not yet. The entire town council was in the room, and Avery knew every single one of them, not that she would point them out to Jake. She didn't know whether or not Jake had learned all their names and faces, although from what little he'd said to her so far, she suspected he had a thick dossier of information on every important individual in town and knew exactly who he should be rubbing elbows with.

It would be interesting to watch how he operated.

But when he suddenly approached two of her sisters, Avery moved so fast she spilled hot coffee on her pants. Brilliant idea, telling Jake in advance that her sisters were the other ones with dogs by their sides. They wouldn't see him coming.

She mentally smacked her forehead with her palm. Even if she had decided not to go into detail, she definitely should have mentioned her earlier meeting with Jake sometime during the dinner conversation these last few days. But it had never seemed the right time because, though it was about Jake, it went beyond his arrival in town and their unexpected meeting at the Meyers' cabin.

If Jake got to her sisters first, before she could explain how she already knew him, who knew what kind of stories *he* would have to tell about their memorable first meeting?

"Jake," she called, causing him to turn around to look at her.

His smile appeared welcoming and genuine. Then again, he believed he had the upper hand. Why wouldn't he be smiling?

"Let me introduce you to two of my sisters," she said, feeling out of breath even though she'd only dashed across the room. "This is Felicity and this is Ruby. Ladies, meet Jake Cutter, who is *visiting* town with his mom and daughter."

Both of her sisters slid her questioning glances, obviously wondering why she was making the introductions to a man who was completely new to town. She could see it in their eyes.

"I ran into him when I was…*out* the other day."

"Funny that you didn't mention him before now," Ruby prodded playfully.

Jake took a step back and clasped at his chest as if he were having a heart attack. "You didn't say anything to your family about my dashing good looks and charming personality? I'm mortally wounded."

Of course he was only teasing, but Avery had to work hard not to roll her eyes at the blatant arrogance behind his words.

"Well, there is that. You are quite good-looking, although you know it's kind of conceited to toot your own horn. Are you telling us you're single?" Felicity asked, bringing color to Jake's cheeks.

As far as Avery was concerned, he deserved whatever he got.

He paused before speaking, clearly taken aback. "Uh… I'm a widower."

"I'm so sorry," Avery said and meant it. She really didn't want to get into Jake's private life in any way, but she'd always been naturally empathetic and hadn't missed the flash of pain and grief that had momentarily crossed his face.

Even a man like Jake deserved her compassion.

"Thank you," he said, his voice tight and his Adam's apple bobbing. "It's been tough raising my daughter on my own, but my mother is a great blessing to me."

"Lottie is a total sweetheart," Avery said.

Again, she noticed sadness creeping into his gaze. But just as quickly as it appeared, his charming smile was back.

"You know," he said, clearly deflecting, "Avery did mention she had sisters when we were talking earlier. She told me to look for the ladies with the dogs at their sides. But she didn't say a thing about how beauty runs in the family."

Ruby's eyes widened, and she threw back her head, laughing out loud. "I do believe this one's a keeper, Avery. You'd better grab him now while you have the opportunity."

"Why would you think—" Avery started to ask, but Jake gave a delighted Texas whoop that caught the attention of most of the people in the room. Now it was Avery who was blushing, her face feeling as if it was on fire.

Why on earth would her sisters get the impression she wanted to date the man? Even without knowing she and Jake were on opposite sides of a property dispute, they knew why Avery would avoid getting tangled up with Jake and his family.

Because even if things were different and they weren't arm wrestling over *her* bed-and-breakfast, Jake had a child. And the fact that Lottie was so precious was even more of a reason for her to steer clear of developing any personal relationship with the Cutter family.

Loving and losing in a romantic relationship was one thing. Loving and losing a man with a family was a whole other thing entirely. She'd been through it once several years ago with a local man named T.J., the only serious relationship she'd ever had, and it would never, ever happen again. Never seeing T.J. after she'd broken up with him was a given, but she'd spent so much time with his son, Oliver, that to suddenly be no longer a part of the boy's life—that was so much harder than she could ever have imagined.

Avery knew she couldn't withstand a second heartbreak.

"I'm here in town for a while doing some work for Marston Enterprises. Have you heard of them?" Jake asked.

Her sisters glanced at each other and shook their heads.

"No, sorry," said Ruby.

"Seriously? It's a huge company. I'm surprised no one around here seems to have heard of us. We have major resorts located in Aspen and Vail and several more around the country."

"Resorts?" Felicity echoed.

"The high-end kind," Avery cut in, noticing her bitter tone only after the words were out of her mouth. "The ones that offer the kind of spa days we could never afford if we saved for a month."

His half smile turned into laughter. "Is that what's bothering you? Tell you what. How about I make sure you all get coupons for an all-expenses-paid spa day on me? Does that sound good?"

Avery narrowed her eyes on him while her sisters cooed in delight and clapped their hands. They hadn't had time to think through the ramifications the way she had. Jake was simply trying to buy their goodwill, and she was having none of it.

He'd have to do a lot better than a spa day. Avery was thinking more of a decision not to use Whispering Pines at all or her cabin in particular.

"Where's your mom and Lottie?" Avery asked, folding her arms across her chest in an unconsciously defensive gesture. She'd rather speak to Elaine than Jake, anyway.

Jake snapped his fingers and winked at her.

"Lottie was getting antsy so my mom took her out to the car. I told them I'd only be another ten minutes, and that was a good fifteen minutes ago. Thanks for reminding me. Nice meeting you, ladies. I'd better run, but I hope we'll be able to talk another time."

"I imagine we will," Avery said under her breath, though honestly, she'd rather not if she could avoid it.

At least Ruby had the decency to wait until Jake was completely out of earshot before she spoke up.

"Do you want to tell us what that was all about?"

Avery feigned ignorance. "What are you talking about?"

"Oh, come on," Ruby pressed. "There was clearly something going on between the two of you. Spill it, girl, because it makes no sense to Felicity and me. He seems like a genuinely nice guy and definitely paid special attention to you, and yet you looked as if you wanted to toss him out on his ear."

"That's not such a bad idea," Avery admitted.

"He said you two already knew each other. When did you meet him?" Ruby asked.

"And where?" Felicity added. "And maybe most important, why didn't you say anything about it? He's too cute to ignore."

"Well, you know how it's been a dream of mine to open a bed-and-breakfast where guests of the service-dog program could stay while they're going through the training program? Recently, I've started putting that dream into action. Lisa Gibbons has been helping me look around for some place I can remodel into a workable B and B."

"That's fantastic news!" Ruby exclaimed. "Why is this the first we've heard of this? You should have told us."

Avery shrugged, and her face heated. "I don't know. Honestly, I guess I just wanted it to be a surprise. You know how I am. I'd rather have all the puzzle pieces fitted together to make a full picture before I go and blurt the news to everyone else."

"So, I take it you found a place you like?" Felicity asked. "Does this have something to do with Jake?"

Avery groaned. "It has everything to do with Jake. Lisa helped me find this absolutely perfect cabin. You probably know the one—the Meyers used to live there? It won't even take that much construction work to make it into a bed-and-breakfast, although admittedly it will take a lot of elbow grease. But that's half the fun, right? I fell in love with it the moment I set eyes on it."

"Let me guess," Felicity said. "That would be the exact spot where Jake and his ginormous company want to open their resort."

"Exactly. He—well, like you said, his company—intends to buy up all the land in that area, including where my cabin sits. And you know what he plans to do with my lovely cabin? Knock it down!"

"I guess that explains the icy wall between the two of you. Can't you convince him to look elsewhere?" Felicity asked.

"Apparently, Marston has already made their final decision. Now it's up to Jake to convince the town council the resort will be a good thing for Whispering Pines and make sure the zoning works for them."

"But apart from your cabin, you don't

think it would be a good idea to build a resort here?"

"I don't know. I want to say no because I'm afraid of what that kind of resort might do to our small town. Yes, it has the potential to bring in new customers to our existing businesses, and that could theoretically be good for the town.

"Or not. From what Jake said, it will be a high-end resort which will draw in the rich and famous, and I can't help but see that going the wrong way. You've been to Aspen. I'm afraid to go into any of the shops there because I might accidentally bump into something and break it, and it would end up costing me my whole year's salary. And I wonder what would happen to all of our local businesses once they build here."

"Well, it could bring in more customers for the locals and benefit everyone," Ruby said hesitantly. "Our shops wouldn't necessarily have to close—just adapt. I can see it working in our favor."

"Or, it could bring in more business for the locals and benefit everyone," Avery echoed petulantly. "Which is why this is so difficult for me."

"Because the real point is the cabin, right? That it's the one you've been waiting and watching for and you don't want to give up on it? A heart thing?"

"Exactly. A heart thing. I took one look at it and I knew it was perfect for me. More so than I can even express in words. Which is why this is so difficult."

"Then, we need to share this situation with the rest of the family and get everyone praying about it."

Shame flooded through Avery. Of course she should include her family. That's what she should have done in the first place, the very day she'd met Jake. She should have shared her burden about the cabin with her family and asked them to pray with her.

Because she might be too small to take on a giant Goliath like Marston Enterprises on her own, but God wasn't.

Tuesday afternoon, Jake decided to take Lottie out for pizza. He'd seen a pizza place on the main street, Lone Elk Avenue, and had tucked the location in the back of his mind. Sharing a pizza together was a tradition they'd had since Lottie was old enough to eat whole foods. Pepperoni pizza with extra cheese was her favorite, so he ordered a whole pepperoni pizza and one extra slice loaded with everything except anchovies for him.

He was really enjoying his time in Whispering Pines. Everyone was so open and friendly with him and his family. He'd spent a lot of time in small towns while traveling for work, but none of them compared to this one. Everyone knew everybody else in a special way, and neighbors really cared for each other. He'd seen youngsters shoveling snow for the elderly, and several folks had stopped by their cabin with welcome packages, even though they would only be in Whispering Pines for a relatively short amount of time.

Sally, the owner of Sally's Pizza, had even come out from the back of the restaurant to introduce herself before personally taking their order.

The bell over the door rang, and Jake automatically glanced up to see who'd entered. To his surprise, it was Avery, and as usual, she had a dog with her, this time a medium-size, golden-haired pup who hopped and swung around in circles, a regular bundle of energy

Jake thought must be difficult to work with. Yet with one word, Avery settled the dog at her side and approached the counter.

"Avery," he called out before he could think better of it.

She turned around, looking dumbstruck. She was probably just as surprised to see him here. It was strange. They couldn't even go get a slice of pizza without bumping into each other.

At least he had Lottie with him this time. His adorable daughter was sure to help make their interaction a little less awkward. Lottie was as cute as they came, with her dark curly hair, button nose and baby-toothed smile. He might be biased, but even if Avery could resist him, she'd surely be won over by Lottie.

And they wouldn't be able to have any serious conversations, which was a big plus.

Avery gave her order to the girl behind the counter and made her way over to where Jake and Lottie were seated.

"Hello! What are you up to?" Avery asked Lottie.

"Eating pizza," Lottie answered excitedly, beaming up at Avery and kicking her legs back and forth on the bench.

"It looks delicious," Avery said. "My favorite kind of pizza is pepperoni, too. With extra cheese, of course."

"Why don't you join us?" Jake asked with his usual grin, hoping for once it would win Avery over.

"Oh, no, I…"

He lifted an eyebrow, waiting for her to come up with an excuse, but she apparently couldn't think of a reasonable explanation for walking away.

"Yeah, okay. I suppose I can join you, but just for a few minutes. I have a truck full of dog food and a kennel of hungry dogs back at the house waiting for me."

"Which dog is this?" Jake asked as Lottie reached out to pet the honey-colored dog.

"Her name is Sissy. She's a golden retriever. We think she's purebred, though we don't know for sure."

"Pretty doggy," Lottie said as Sissy lapped up her attention, nosing her and licking her palm.

"She sure is. She has a gorgeous coat, doesn't she? Sissy is currently my favorite, actually. I've been doing a lot of work with her. She was abandoned as a puppy—dumped on our doorstep, if you can believe it. I had to bottle-feed her every two hours around the clock until she was old enough to eat wet solids, so I feel especially close to her. She's my baby."

A smile lingered on her lips, one of the few genuine smiles Jake had seen. He noted that she was especially pretty when she wasn't stressed, when she was talking about something she really cared about.

"How old is she now?" Jake asked. Her dogs appeared to be a safe topic to speak about.

It occurred to him a second time that since she appeared so relaxed and open, he might be able to use this opportunity to try to come to some kind of business agreement, but he quickly brushed those thoughts aside in favor of simply getting to know her better. Besides, this was his special time with Lottie, not time for talking business.

"A little over two years old. As you probably saw when we first entered the restaurant, she still has a lot of puppy energy, but her training is nearly complete. I'll hate to see her go when the time comes, but she's going to be a real blessing to someone special."

"I'm sure she will be. You said your program does more than train dogs for the blind. What else do they do?"

"You'd be surprised at the range of assistance a service dog can offer," she said. She paused to thank Sally when she brought out her slice of pepperoni with extra cheese and a slice of meat pizza all boxed up to go.

She blew on the pizza, then took a bite, dabbing her mouth with a napkin before she continued.

"We've placed a dog for a person who is deaf, several hospital-therapy dogs, search-and-rescue and crisis-therapy dogs, among others. Recently, my sister Molly got married. Her stepson is on the autism spectrum, and one of our dogs really fit the bill to help him understand and process his world."

"You trained a dog to help a boy with autism? Wow, I've never even heard of such a thing."

"We've done some psychiatric service-dog work in the past, but this dog, a Great Dane named Rufus, was amazing. We had no idea. Molly was just out with Rufus one day when he suddenly showed us where he belonged. Without prompting, he took to little Judah as if he'd been specially made for him. Everyone could see it."

"That is incredible." Jake could barely put his amazement into words. He'd never even imagined dogs could be so useful.

"I know, right?" Avery actually smiled at him before biting into her pizza again. Another real smile, not the tight, gritted-teeth variety she'd given him since they'd met.

He tried to ignore what that smile did to his insides. He had to stay focused on the end goal, and that wasn't Avery. If anything, the woman was standing right in his way, blocking the puck, so to speak.

Suddenly, Sissy, who had been lying down quietly next to Avery's foot, whined and wiggled over closer to the other side of the bench where the child was sitting, repeatedly nudging Lottie's chest with her nose and licking her chin.

With a curious gleam in her eye, Avery called her off, but Sissy ignored her and continued her ministrations to the little girl, completely focused on Lottie.

"That's odd," Avery said, her brow lowering. "It's not at all like Sissy to ignore a direct command. Something's wrong."

As he stared as his daughter, Jake's face heated as he watched the dog and realized in hindsight he probably should not have let Lottie pet Sissy before she'd finished her pizza, or at least he ought to insist she go wash her hands now that the dog was touching her again right in the middle of their meal.

What kind of father was he, anyway?

It didn't really surprise him that she was more interested in the dog than the pizza, having begged for one so many times since she'd learned how to speak. But he ought to be more aware of things like hand-washing. It was times like this that made him feel as if he was never going to be able to live up to becoming the kind of parent Lottie deserved. And although he couldn't imagine why it mattered, he didn't want to come off looking like a slacker dad to Avery.

"Daddy?" Lottie said, her voice high, squeaky and frightened.

"Yes, honey?" he said, immediately locking his attention on his daughter. Something in the tone of her voice alerted him.

It was no longer about the dog, although Sissy was still persistently nuzzling her. Lottie had a strange look on her face—an expression Jake knew all too well.

"I don't feel so good."

"Sweetheart?" Jake asked.

Sissy barked and nudged Lottie again. Suddenly, his darling girl stiffened like a board and clutched at the edge of the table, her face blanching as, in her spasmodic movements, her arm bumped her glass, spilling water all across the table.

Because he was sitting across the table from her, Jake couldn't immediately react. But before he could so much as move a muscle, Avery had scooped Lottie into her arms. She knelt down on the floor with her and tenderly laid her on her side. Avery folded her jacket and gently placed it under Lottie's head, her knees on either side of her and her hands steady near Lottie's cheeks so she wouldn't hurt herself.

Avery's expression was full of concern, but she appeared to know what she was doing, even though Jake hadn't yet offered a word of explanation as to what was going on with his daughter.

"It's okay, Lottie. Your daddy and I are right here." Avery spoke loudly, reassuringly and evenly. "You're going to be all right, sweetheart. We're not going anywhere."

Jake dropped to his knees beside his daughter and gently stroked her shoulder. He knew she could hear him, even if she couldn't directly respond to his voice. "Daddy's here. Daddy loves you. Hang in there, sweetie. It's okay. You're going to be just fine."

Suddenly, the dog was down beside them, wiggling underneath Jake's arm so she could be closer to Lottie, stretching herself out at the child's side.

Instead of freaking out at the child's uncomfortable movements and darting away from the little girl, Sissy put her head across Lottie's chest and gently licked her chin until the seizure had come to an end.

Was there such a thing as an epilepsy-support dog? Jake had never heard of such a thing, but then, he hadn't ever heard of an autism-support dog, either. The way Sissy was acting right now, it seemed as though the dog instinctively knew what was happening. Now that he thought of it, Sissy had alerted them even before Lottie showed signs that she was going to have a seizure.

Finally, Lottie's seizure wound down, and

Jake met Avery's compassionate gaze as she stroked the hair away from his daughter's forehead.

"Epilepsy?" Avery whispered.

His heart aching until he thought it might burst from pain, Jake nodded.

# *Chapter Four*

Avery ran Sissy through the agility course at A New Leash on Love, which included jumps, tubes, ladders, balance beams and weaving poles. There were several ways to run through the course, so the dogs didn't get too used to any one pattern and always had to pay attention to their handlers for instructions.

Though for Colorado it was a mild winter day in late January, Avery could still see her breath as she jogged alongside Sissy and gestured her through the course for the third time, encouraging her to run through a long, curved tunnel that was one of the dog's favorites. When Avery had first left the house just after lunch, she'd worn an orange Broncos puffer vest over her thick white Aran Celticknot sweater, but she'd since divested herself of the coat. Agility was a great workout for humans as well as dogs, and she was feeling the burn.

Though Sissy had lots of puppy energy going today, she wasn't quite as mentally focused as she usually was, something the dog needed to be in order to pay attention to Avery and successfully run the course. Twice in one run, she veered off in a different direction after an obstacle and dashed the wrong way, and Avery had to whistle and gesture to bring her back in line.

Sissy wasn't the only one veering off course today. Avery's mind was likewise all over the place, and she couldn't seem to pull it back to attention, no matter what she did or how hard she tried. No doubt Sissy, as with any sensitive dog, was picking up on her human's anxiety, and that was part of the problem as to why the normally obedient pup was so off-kilter today.

Avery rued the day Jake Cutter had entered her life and made things so complicated. She *so* wanted to dislike him and his fancy suits, polished cowboy boots, shiny red Mustang and toothy-grinned charm, but how could she, when she'd seen what a loving, compassionate father he was to Lottie?

If only she hadn't noticed. But she had. There was a caring heart beating under that annoyingly swaggering exterior.

This was not good.

*Really* not good.

A warning beacon went off in her own heart. She needed to figure out how to take on Jake and his company over her bed-and-breakfast cabin—not only for herself, but for the sake of the town itself. It was crucial that she maintain her emotional distance from him so she could keep her head on straight to fight the good fight and win.

What she did not need to do was get any closer to him and sweet Lottie. She knew herself well enough to know how easily her mind and heart could be turned. It had happened before, leading to the worst heartbreak of her life—one which she never intended to repeat. And the best way to avoid becoming involved with Jake was to stay as far away from him and his family as possible.

Brilliant idea, and yet she'd done the exact opposite of that. Directly after Lottie had had her epilepsy episode, Avery had blurted out that the little girl could come visit Sissy at the farm and see the other rescue dogs, as well as the petting zoo, and they'd made specific plans to do so. Of course, she'd already made that invitation to Jake's mom that day at church.

Suddenly an idea occurred to her.

She might be able to salvage this disaster of a day after all and make it work to her benefit. Jake would be relaxed spending time with his family and not thinking about his job, right? So, wouldn't that be the perfect time to charge in and try to work things out to her benefit? Show him firsthand the benefits of small-town life?

She saw the dust on the dirt driveway before she actually saw his car. He was still driving around in that completely impractical red Mustang, which he must be taking through the car wash at least once a day, as it remained in sparkling condition as always. Yet, the impracticality of such a vehicle was glaringly obvious, not only because he was driving around in a mountain town with plenty of bumpy dirt roads, but with the knowledge that today he had a child with him. Had the man never heard of a child-safe sports utility vehicle?

At least he was driving with some modicum of caution this time and not rip-roaring down the drive at a race car's pace as he'd done last time she'd seen him behind the wheel.

Even though her anxiety instantly shot through the roof the moment she saw his car, it actually didn't take much to force a smile on her face as she called Sissy to her side and put her in a down-stay position.

Maybe it was because she wasn't facing Jake alone. So far, she'd managed to always have others with her when she was around him, and though she knew she needed to guard her heart, she especially liked Elaine and Lottie.

She smiled as Elaine unfolded herself from the passenger seat with a great deal more grace than Avery thought she herself would have been able to do. She imagined she probably would have been all awkward arms and legs at best. The sports car wasn't exactly meant for ease of use. And it only took Jake a moment to unlatch a wiggling Lottie from her car seat so she could crawl from the back seat and into his arms.

Lottie's eyes were wide as she took in the tree farm and all of the dogs running around in the pen behind Avery. Avery suspected Winslow's Woodlands would have nearly the same impact on the little girl, being from the city, as going to Disneyland, full of excitement and fun and new experiences.

"Sissy!" Lottie squealed, opening her arms to the dog lying obediently at Avery's heel.

Avery released Sissy from her down-stay position, and the dog promptly ran into Lottie's arms, giving her a welcome nuzzle under her chin.

"I told Sissy you were coming today," she told Lottie with a laugh. "As you can tell, she's been waiting for you all morning and is super excited to see you."

"We're happy to be here, as well," Elaine answered enthusiastically, since Lottie was busy rolling around in the grass with the dog, giggling and squealing in delight. "Lottie's been chattering about it since breakfast this morning. It was so kind of you to invite us."

"I'm glad you could all come," Avery said

and was surprised to find she genuinely meant it.

*Mostly.*

She didn't miss the way Jake's eyebrows shot up at her declaration. Clearly, he didn't believe she could put aside their differences in order to give his daughter a day she wouldn't quickly forget.

As if she would be so petty. Okay, well, she could be, especially with a man with as much bluster as Jake, but she had it in her to put her own feelings aside, with the Lord's help.

She'd show him. She loved children, and Lottie was especially dear to her after seeing her suffer through a grand mal seizure with such bravery.

Not that it would be easy for her, but not for the reasons Jake might believe. He would have no idea just how hard it would really be for her to be here interacting with his family. She'd promised herself she'd avoid situations like this—spending time with an attractive man who was also a father to a darling child.

As she well knew, that way led only to double heartbreak.

But it wasn't as if this was a date or anything, or even close to something romantic.

After all, his mother was here accompanying them. A chaperone and a child should be more than enough to keep them behaving properly.

He just stuffed his hands in the front pockets of his what must have been brand-spanking-new black denim jeans and rocked back on the heels of his boots, a heartwarming half smile lingering on his lips and a sparkle in his eyes. She had to admit he looked nice in his jeans and comfortable yellow-and-black checked flannel shirt, a marked difference from the suits he usually wore.

Nice.

And relaxed.

Far more than she was.

"We've got a lot to see today, but how about we start by my showing you around the dog-rescue center," Avery suggested. "And then we can head over to the tree farm and petting zoo. Do you want to see some more doggies, Lottie? We've got lots of them."

"That sounds delightful," exclaimed Elaine, sounding almost as excited as her granddaughter. Lottie bounded around, pumping her arms, a little ball of energy the puppies were sure to pick up on.

Jake was watching his daughter, a smile on his face.

"This is our dog run," Avery said, pointing behind her to a huge, fenced yard that stretched beyond where her eyes could see. Inside were dozens of dog toys—everything from squeaky toys to tennis balls to rope pulls—a full agility course and a couple of plastic swimming pools filled to the rim with water.

"Swim?" Lottie asked eagerly.

Avery laughed. "Maybe another time. That water is freezing cold right now. We have to keep an eye on it in the wintertime, or it freezes over. The pools are actually for some of our dogs who especially like water. Right now we have a couple of Labrador retrievers, a big, fluffy Newfoundland and a standard Poodle who absolutely love getting wet, winter or summer, even when the water is freezing cold. And there's Sissy, of course. She's a golden retriever and splashes around with the best of them. We clean out the pools every day, but it doesn't take much for them to get dirty and muddy again, especially this time of year."

"So, how do you keep 'em clean?" Jake asked.

"The pools or the dogs?" Avery quipped back, somehow unable to stop from smiling at him.

"What with all the dogs running around on the lawn, for some reason I'm picturing a dog wash similar to a car wash, with twirling brushes and tons of soapsuds."

"Not such a bad idea," Avery said with a genuine laugh—something she hadn't really expected to do much of today. "I could see that working. Maybe I can run that idea by my brother Sharpe. He does most of the building and tinkering around here. As it is right now, all the dogs get scrubbed up and hosed down in a warm shower made specially for that purpose and then blow-dried every evening."

"I'm picturing a doggy salon here. Sounds like a lot of work," Jake said with a chuckle.

"Oh, it is, believe me. But it's a joy working with the dogs. They show their appreciation. And it's totally worth it when we are able to pair one of our pups up with an owner in need. Watching a service dog discover its job is like nothing else in this world."

"Jake told me what happened at Sally's Pizza," Elaine said. "He couldn't believe the way Sissy reacted, how she responded to Lottie without having to be told what to do."

"She was amazing," agreed Avery. "It's exactly what we look for in our dogs. They are mostly rescue dogs when they come into our facilities. We give them lots of love, put them through basic and advanced training, and then start watching for them to show us what they're meant to do with their lives."

Avery wanted to say more—that the Lord was speaking to her heart about Sissy, and that she'd like to start training her for Lottie with her epilepsy. But how could that be, when another part of her was screaming that she wanted nothing whatsoever to do with Lottie's father?

She couldn't train Sissy and Lottie together without Jake being there and taking part. Yet, there was no way for them to resolve the situation between them with the Meyers' land, and for that reason, Avery remained silent.

It wasn't Lottie's fault her father and Avery were very much on opposite sides of the fence in this quarrel, and yet Avery wasn't quite ready to let go of her dream house. But she needed to put aside her personal feelings, especially if it meant helping a little girl. She'd need to mentally prepare herself to make the offer, though.

"Let me show you where our dogs stay during the night and cold winter storms, and give you a glimpse of our indoor training facility, as well," she said instead, gesturing to a building made of brick with maroon siding and gray shingles. "You'll get to see my sisters Ruby and Felicity in action. I think they're both training dogs this afternoon."

Jake whistled under his breath. "That's a big building. How many dogs do you house there?"

"It depends," Avery said as she opened the door to the training facility and gestured them inside. "Usually somewhere between five and ten, but we've had up to twenty, and there have been a couple of times we've found or been given a mama with a litter of pups needing our assistance. We do what we can for them."

Everyone, even Lottie, quieted as they entered the training facility, where Ruby and Felicity were putting dogs through their motions. When her sisters saw her with Jake and his family, they immediately stopped and put the dogs they were working with into a down-stay, then approached the Cutters with friendly smiles all around.

"Welcome," Felicity said. "Have you all come to watch us train today?"

"Not really," Avery said. "Maybe for a minute or two. Mostly I'm just showing them around the farm and rescue today."

"Don't miss the petting zoo," Felicity said enthusiastically.

"No, of course not," Avery said, wishing she had a moment to speak with her sisters without Jake and his family overhearing. "Felicity, maybe you can show them what you're doing with Roxie," she suggested, linking her arm with Ruby in an unspoken bid for support.

"Sure," said Felicity, calling Roxie to her side. The dog automatically rounded about Felicity's feet and sat at her heel. "This dog is really cool, Lottie. Isn't she funny looking, almost like a Teddy bear?"

Lottie squealed in delight while nodding.

"Roxie can do all kinds of things," Felicity continued. "Would you like to see her open a refrigerator door and bring you back a cold pop?"

Felicity glanced at Jake, who nodded his assent, his expression as full of surprise and curiosity as his daughter's was.

Meanwhile, Avery pulled Ruby aside.

"What's up, sis?" Ruby asked, keeping her voice low and her gaze on what was happening across the room.

"I'm thinking about Sissy," Avery said in a low whisper. "You should have seen it. She naturally responded to Lottie the other day when she had an epileptic seizure. I'd like to train her specifically for Lottie."

Ruby's gaze widened. "I'm all for that. It's always exciting when one of our dogs shows us what she's destined for. But doesn't it put you in an awkward position, with Jake being her dad and all? You two are still arguing over the Meyers' land, right?"

Avery shrugged. "Very much so. And I've been doing a lot of research, which may help me win my case against him. There are a lot of endangered plants and animals around here, along with lots of Rocky Mountain Columbines growing on the Meyers' lot. I'm not giving up on my dream so fast."

She paused and watched the dog-training display for a moment. "But that's not what I'm talking about right now," she continued. "There's a little girl over there who needs the help that I believe Sissy can provide. I have to be mature enough to set aside my feelings about Lottie's father to do the right thing, to do what's best for Lottie."

Ruby put a hand on her forearm. "Of course you do. I'm so proud of you. You are—mature enough to handle it, I mean. I applaud you for putting aside your own feelings this way. I'll talk with the others, but it sounds to me as if Sissy is exactly what Lottie needs to help her with her episodes. We'll put her on the whiteboard starting today for special training in epilepsy events. Do you want to be the one to approach Jake with the idea, or would you rather one of us do it?"

Avery sighed, very much wanting to take herself out of the equation as much as possible. But that was ridiculous and shallow, and besides, she wanted to be the one to train Sissy. She already knew Jake better than the others, and she suspected they would be spending a lot more time together before he either gave up on Marston's plans and left town or else squashed her dreams for a bed-and-breakfast like a tiny bug, which seemed more and more likely as time went on.

"No, let me be the one to speak to him," she said, wishing she sounded stronger than she felt. "I've already been working with Sissy on all of her basic and advanced training. It only makes sense for me to be the one to do it."

Lottie ran up, her face beaming as she held out a cold can of soda. "Roxie got this for me. Right out of the refrigerator. She used her mouth and a rope. So cool!"

"I'll have to agree with her there," Jake said, walking toward her with his usual swagger, his hands in his jeans pockets and a grin on his face. "I can't believe Roxie opened the fridge all by herself. What a smart pup you've got here. In fact, I think you've got a whole lot of superdogs here."

"Oh, don't you know it! Roxie also turns lights on and off, among other things," Ruby said. "And she can be used to steady a person trying to stand up if they have difficulty with their balance."

Jake's eyebrows shot upward. "Color me impressed."

Avery's eyebrows did the exact opposite, lowering over her eyes in annoyance. The man was far too handsome for his own good when something as simple as moving his eyebrows made her stomach flutter.

Or maybe it was just that she hadn't had lunch.

Yeah. That had to be it. Because she was absolutely *not* going to let her head be turned by a man like Jake Cutter.

She changed her expression before anyone else could see she'd been affected by Jake's posturing. "I'm sure Ruby and Felicity would be happy to have you all come and watch them train with the dogs sometime," she said. "It's really quite interesting, given the number and ages of dogs we have who are all learning different parts of the program. However, right now, why don't we continue the tour. Let's check out the dog kennel, where they spend their evenings."

Jake's eyes widened and he whistled. A New Leash on Love had a whole other definition for the term *dog kennel*. He'd been expecting chain-link fences and wooden doghouses. Maybe larger than normal, given that the whole operation tended to be that way, but he hadn't been the least bit prepared for what the program actually used.

It was one very large room that looked more like what Marston Enterprises offered its guests in the lobby than anything remotely resembling a dog kennel.

Several couches lined the room, as well as a couple of deep armchairs where various breeds of dogs both large and small were stretched out, their tongues lolling as they peacefully slept. Dog beds and pillows were haphazardly tossed about the room at random intervals. There was a toy box entirely full of various chew toys, which apparently the dogs could use whenever they chose.

They even had a television that offered soft background noise.

"You gave your dogs a television?" Jake asked, lifting his cowboy hat and scratching his head. He felt as if he'd just stepped into *The Twilight Zone*, where dogs had been anthropomorphized and were living a life of luxury.

"You don't have a TV at your house?" Avery parried lightly.

"Well, sure we do, but—"

"And so does everyone else I know. People these days almost always have their televisions on running in the background, even when they aren't paying attention to whatever is on. We want our dogs completely prepared for the environments in which they'll be living. As part of our adoption process, we vet everyone who wants one of our dogs to make sure their new family member will be staying inside the house, whether they end up as service dogs or simply beloved family pets. With the pups being able to come in here and relax when they're not working, the dogs are already comfortable with the sights, sounds and smells of a typical living room, and it will be easier for them to adjust."

Jake snorted. "This looks more like a hotel suite, if you ask me."

Avery grinned. "Very much so. And my sisters and I are the concierges. No hors d'oeuvres or anything like that, but we make sure they get regular treats at various times of the day, whether or not they will end up passing the program as service dogs."

"So, you adopt out dogs, as well as train them, if for some reason they don't work out for you?" Jake asked. He was beginning to realize just how blessed these pups were. They may have come from bad situations, but they'd just landed in doggy playland. Even if they didn't end up being service dogs, it looked to him as if the Winslows went above and beyond taking care of their charges.

"A little more than half our dogs are adopted out to regular families to be family pets. Not every dog who comes into our center is meant for service in the traditional sense, and many of them—I don't want to say they fail in any way—they're just not quite what we're looking for in terms of a work program. Service dogs must have a strong drive—food or play, for example—which we can use when we train them for their special jobs.

"Other dogs just want to love on their people and be couch potatoes or running buddies or snuggle bugs, and that's okay, too. Better than okay. We've made dozens of wonderful matches with families just looking for the perfect pet. Our goal is to try to take the best possible care of the dogs we have as they come in. The way we look at it is God gives us every one of these special pups. Even if they don't end up as service dogs, they'll all have been trained in basic commands using the American Kennel Club's Canine Good Citizen program. It's our ministry, and the dogs we put out prove that."

"Do you actively search out dogs to train, or do they come to you?" Jake's mother asked, sitting on one of the couches between a few of the dogs, who immediately scooched to make room for her and then curled up against her and gave her plenty of love, nuzzling her with their noses and licking her chin. Lottie crawled on her grandmother's lap, delighted by all the canine attention she received as one of the smaller dogs snuggled on her lap.

"It depends on how many service dogs we're training and what we discover our biggest needs are at any given moment. Occasionally, we visit local shelters and look for dogs that might specifically fit into our service program. We have detailed tests we use to see if the dog has the correct drive to make a go of it. Sometimes they are motivated by food. Other times all it takes to maintain their interest is their favorite toy, so they feel like they are always playing a game.

"So, to answer your question, yes, we're always on the lookout, although not always actively so. Mostly, God provides. It's an unfortunate fact that there are far more dogs that need to be rescued than there are people willing to open their hearts to these precious pups."

"Well, I've got to say I am thoroughly impressed with everything you've got going here. You and your siblings have done a magnificent job with this training facility, and especially with these sweet dogs," Elaine said.

Jake agreed, although he didn't say so aloud. His life would be much easier if he could set Avery firmly in the enemy camp, but there was no way to do that when she was so incredibly kind and compassionate. The way she spoke about her dogs and her ministry, he could tell she had a good heart. Which led to him believe she most likely had a valid reason for fighting for the house she wanted to be her bed-and-breakfast. Something connected to the Winslow's business, perhaps.

He really didn't want to ask for details. The less he knew about Avery and her situation, the better for him. Usually he tried to get into the heads of those opposing him, but he was scared to death to go there with Avery.

When he and his mother first made plans

to tour Winslow's Woodlands and A New Leash on Love with Avery as their guide, he'd seriously considered not accompanying them. He had a ton of other things to get done besides spend a day trailing around a tree farm. But idiot that he was, he'd thought he might learn something he could use against Avery in his fight to close the Marston Enterprises deal. But not only had she flipped that whole thought over on him and made him realize all the good she was doing for people, but it showed a major defect in his own character even to consider undercutting Avery.

He'd learned a lot about her, all right.

The only problem was, none of it was good—or rather, *everything* about her was good. How was he going to win a fight like that?

Did he even want to?

## Chapter Five

"Next stop, our petting zoo," Avery said brightly, leading the way down to the barn. She was really excited for Lottie to spend some time with their variety of animals. After seeing the little girl with Sissy, she was certain Lottie would love petting all the farm animals. "We've got everything from alpacas and donkeys to sheep, goats and pigs. There's even a friendly Shetland pony who adores children."

"Did you hear that, honey? They have a little horsey to pet," Jake said tenderly in his velvety Texas drawl that made Avery want to melt. There was just something about the way he spoke that wasn't entirely fair to the female population. His voice was as smooth and rich as warm honey—and he knew how to use it.

The walk from the training center to the petting zoo was a long one for a three-year-old, and Jake had swept Lottie into his arms for the trek.

She couldn't help but notice how strong he was, but really, any woman with eyes in her head would have to admit to appreciating his broad shoulders and tight muscles, especially since he was so gently toting his adorable, curly-haired daughter in those arms.

Avery realized she needed to get out more. Go on a few dates. It had clearly been too long since she'd been in a romantic relationship if she found herself somehow unexplainably attracted to a man who was technically her mortal enemy—especially a man who wore cuff links and drove a red Mustang down dirt roads as if it were a race car.

*Sooo* not her type.

A nice, quiet, humble cowboy with deep country roots. That's what she needed. Someone who understood and lived her small-town lifestyle. Unfortunately for her, she'd grown up with all the nice, quiet, humble country cowboys in the area, and either she had already dated all the men her age or else they felt more like brothers to her.

How ironic that the one man to come skidding into her life to shake her up was a man like Jake Cutter. He might be great father material, but in his career working for Marston Enterprises, he was exploitive and pushy, and she should never forget about that. Not for one single second. As long as she kept her head on straight, she could handle this.

"Horses are one of her favorite animals," Elaine elaborated. "She has a stuffed horse named Star she sleeps with every night."

"That's wonderful," Avery exclaimed. "I can't wait to introduce you to our pony. The Shetland is brand-new. Frost just brought him in last week, and we haven't had the opportunity to name him yet. He's a bay—brown in color with a dark mane—and believe it or not, he has a white star on his forehead. Hey, Lottie, what do you think about us naming our pony Star? Would you like that?"

Suddenly shy, Lottie buried her head in Jake's shoulder, but Avery heard a muffled "Yes, please." It was so cute how polite she always was, even when she was unsettled.

"Star it is, then. I think that's a wonderful

name. Thank you for helping us name him, Lottie."

"Welcome," Lottie murmured.

Elaine chuckled. "She's not usually so reserved. I think perhaps it's a bit overwhelming seeing everything all at once. There's an awful lot to interest a little girl at this farm."

Oh, no. Avery suddenly felt horrible and wanted to kick herself for her error. She hadn't even thought of the breadth of the tour from Lottie's point of view, other than that she'd no doubt be excited about meeting the dogs and all of the other animals on their farm. But such an experience was bound to overwhelm a little girl's senses after a while.

She was only three years old. And Winslow's Woodlands—not to mention the service-dog program—was enormous, especially to a little one. No wonder she was hiding her face in her daddy's shoulder.

"Of course this is getting to be too much for her," Avery quickly agreed. "I'm so sorry. I should have thought of that."

"It's not your fault," Jake countered. "It isn't as if you'd automatically know how much a three-year-old can handle on any given day. I'm still learning this parenting thing, and I do it twenty-four hours a day, every day."

"Look, there's no reason we have to do and see everything today. Do you want to skip the petting zoo and do it some other time? We've also got a nice sleigh ride on Saturday afternoons. You all are always welcome to come by, and we can pick it up later. However it works out for you is fine with me. Just give me a call when you'd like to come by."

"No," exclaimed Lottie, lifting her head. "I don't want to go. I want to see the horsey."

Avery chuckled. "Okay, then. We'll be sure to do that today. And then we can play it by ear as to how much more we do with the rest of the petting zoo."

Jake patted Lottie's back and noisily kissed her cheek. It was so cute, Avery's heart did some serious acrobatics.

"It's okay, sweetie," he said. "We won't leave without seeing the horsey."

He switched his gaze to Elaine. "It's not her nap time," he said thoughtfully. "We haven't had lunch yet. Maybe she's hungry. I guess I should have thought to pack us lunch."

Avery glanced around, considering what to do. Suddenly, an idea struck her, and she wondered why she hadn't thought of it in the first place.

"Tell you what. We have a lovely picnic area over by the creek." She pointed in the direction of which she was speaking. "There's a playset for Lottie with swings and a slide. Why don't you three head on over there and take a nice break, while I run back to the house and make us some sandwiches and fresh lemonade for a picnic? I think it's mild enough out today to enjoy the winter weather."

"I'll help you," Jake offered, placing Lottie on the ground. Elaine reached out and took her granddaughter's hand.

"There's no need." The words immediately flew from Avery's mouth without forethought. The last thing she wanted to do was be alone with Jake, even for a short time, inside the cozy kitchen.

She had to admit she was surprised when Jake looked taken aback—a little hurt, even, although he quickly masked his emotions with a lazy smile. For the first time, she'd reached him emotionally—really reached him—and it was over sandwiches. Go figure. She attempted to clarify why she'd been so short with him. "What I mean to say is, why don't you stay out here and enjoy the day with your family?"

"I don't mind. Really. I'd like to help you with the sandwiches." He turned and met her eyes, locking his gaze with hers.

She swallowed hard. He wasn't making this easy on her to reject him. It was either yield to his request or make a scene with his mother and daughter within hearing distance. Neither option appeared the least bit attractive to her, but she had to choose one over the other.

"We can discuss the situation with your… uh, the bed-and-breakfast while we're putting the sandwiches together," he suggested.

Oh, now that was just *so* much better.

But then again, maybe it was, because she was experiencing this wild chemistry with Jake, and she didn't *want* to be noticing him. Not that way. But for some inexplicable reason, no matter what she did, she found her gaze drifting to him. Watching the way he walked, smiled, interacted with his mother and Lottie.

Perhaps a good argument and a reminder of precisely what Jake stood for was exactly what they needed right now to shut down those unwanted emotions for good.

And good riddance to them.

"All right," she conceded with a sigh. "Is that okay with you, Elaine, if Jake joins me to help make lunch?"

"Absolutely," Elaine answered. "Lottie and I will give the swings and the slides a go while you two work on the sandwiches. We'll get all our wiggles out. It's just what we need. You two take your time, and don't rush on our account."

Avery wasn't sure about the mischievous glance Elaine gave her son, nor the smile he returned. Was that a hint of a blush on his cheeks?

Jake gestured Avery ahead of him and placed his palm on the small of her back as they walked up the path toward the house. She supposed it was a natural and gentlemanly thing to do, but she felt as awkward, as if she was a teenager on her very first date. Her nerves were nipping like a pool of snapping turtles.

She needed to get over herself—and Jake— and fast.

She breathed a sigh of relief when they

entered the kitchen and she had a reason to move away from him. She left him at the counter while she opened the refrigerator and started taking out items to prepare sandwiches.

"If you have any tomatoes, I'll slice 'em," Jake offered. He slipped the chef's knife from the butcher's block and examined it for a moment before returning it to the block and settling on the bread knife with a serrated edge. Avery set a wood cutting board in front of him and placed two large, ripe tomatoes on top.

"Does Lottie like tomatoes?" she asked, wondering if she should grab another one from the vegetable crisper.

"Not so much," Jake answered with a grin. "She says they're squishy and yucky in her mouth."

"I suppose they are. Squishy, I mean. I think they're an acquired taste. I didn't like them when I was a kid, either. What about your mom?"

"Oh, definitely. Mom likes pretty much everything on her sandwiches, just like I do. The thicker the layers, the better."

"Let's see here. I have deli meat we can

use. Is turkey okay, or would you rather have roast beef?"

"Mmm. Yes and yes, if you don't mind too much. Mom and Lottie enjoy turkey, but my mouth is watering over the thought of roast beef."

"No problem. As far as I'm concerned, you can have both." Avery pulled the deli meats from the meat drawer and tossed them on the counter, followed by bread, lettuce, presliced cheddar cheese, mayonnaise and mustard. "Anything else you like? Living in a house full of siblings does have its advantages when it comes to a well-stocked refrigerator."

"Everything looks perfect to me." He moved over to the sink to wash the tomatoes, casually slinging a dish towel over his shoulder and humming under his breath as he rinsed the tomatoes clean and dried them off.

Avery basted the bread with mayonnaise and mustard and watched Jake work. Although it was hard to imagine the man who'd shown up to town in a suit worth more than she made in a year preparing his own meals, he appeared completely at home in the country kitchen, as if he often cooked for himself. He had mentioned he'd done a semester of culinary arts training, but that was a far cry from making deli sandwiches. Yet another fact in the mystery that was Jake Cutter.

"Where will I find the lemonade mix?" he asked when the tomatoes were neatly sliced and he'd hand-washed the knife and returned it to the butcher's block.

"It's in the pantry, on the second shelf down on the right-hand side." She pointed to the walk-in pantry with the tip of the butter knife she was using to swipe the mayo and mustard onto the bread.

He rummaged through the pantry and returned with the lemonade mix and a sealed container labeled *sugar*. Meanwhile, Avery pulled a plastic pitcher from the nearby cupboard and a measuring cup and mixing spoon from a drawer.

"So…" he said, drawing out the word as he placed the lemonade-mix container on the counter next to her. There was plenty of room for him to work on the counter, but he'd chosen to majorly invade her space. Or maybe that was just his MO. In either case, he was much too close, his shoulder nearly touching hers, and her breath caught in her throat as she inhaled a heady whiff of his crisp aftershave.

"So?" she asked when he didn't continue his thought.

"Have you—that is, I don't want to ruin our day, and I'm not quite sure how to ask this."

"Just spit it out," she said, sensing his next words were going to be something she didn't want to hear. Perhaps it would have been better to tell him not to bother, that she already knew what he was going to ask and he wasn't going to like the answer.

He cleared his throat and wiped his hands on the dish towel flung across his broad shoulder. "Have you found someplace that will suit for your bed-and-breakfast?"

Jake regretted asking the question the moment he said it.

Avery stopped spreading mustard over a piece of bread and turned to him, the knife in her hand pointed rather threateningly toward his chest. For a moment, her mouth moved, but nothing came out.

He just kept watching the knife. It was a butter knife and really couldn't do much harm other than splattering his shirt with mustard. Since he was just wearing a flannel shirt and not one of his expensive suits, it wasn't really a big deal, but he couldn't help but be alarmed by the way her face reddened to the color of the tomatoes he'd just sliced.

"Y-yes," she finally stammered. "Yes, I did."

"Oh, good. I'm really glad to hear it." He smiled encouragingly and let out the breath he'd been holding. Funny that he'd been holding his breath, as well. He hadn't realized.

This was good news. If she'd found somewhere else where she could focus her dreams, there would no longer be any reason to have trouble between them. They might even become friends, right? He found he liked the idea—maybe more than he should, all things considered.

Except the expression on Avery's face wasn't exactly friendly. Or even relieved, which she should be if she'd found someplace else to remodel into a bed-and-breakfast. Instead, her gaze was filled with a fiery determination, and she'd set her jaw in such a way that didn't bode well for him.

"The Meyers' cabin," she said in a clipped monotone. "That's where I've chosen to open my bed-and-breakfast. It's perfect for my needs. I'm going to remodel the Meyers' cabin. I've already got blueprints, and I'm making some major plans for it."

He'd just assumed—wrongly, obviously—that once she realized what she was up against, which he was certain he'd made clear to her, she'd go with a plan B and find somewhere else to build her dreams. It wasn't as if there weren't dozens of cabins in and around Whispering Pines. But for some unknown reason, she thought she had to have this particular one?

No one could fight a huge corporation like Marston Enterprises and win. She must know that.

But the look in her eyes suggested otherwise.

And he hated to be the one to let her down.

"Avery," he said softly. "Surely—"

"Surely nothing," Avery snapped back, turning back to the sandwich she was preparing, splashing mustard across the bread with a great deal more force than was necessary, and getting it on the countertop. "I don't want to talk about it anymore right now."

"I really think we should." Although he

couldn't imagine why, he instinctively reached out to her, but she jerked away from him.

He didn't know what he could say to make things better. There really wasn't anything to say. He was quite literally working for the enemy. And yet he desperately wanted to rescue this conversation in some way. Turn it around and make things better.

They'd been getting along so well all day, and even, for that matter, the other day when they'd been out for pizza and she'd been there for Lottie during her episode.

There'd been moments…

That, he realized, was his problem.

The moments.

"Okay, well, what do you want me to say?" she demanded. "I found the perfect spot for my bed-and-breakfast, and you and your big company want to take it away from me. Has that changed in any way since we first talked about it?"

"Well, no, but… Avery, this isn't personal. You know that, right?"

"It feels personal."

"Only if you make it that way."

Tears filled her eyes, but she quickly

dashed them away. "Grrr. I hate it that I cry when I'm angry."

He hated seeing her cry at all.

"Just so you know," she continued, pressing her palms to her eyes to staunch the flow of angry tears, "I'm going to fight you and your gigantic company over this. Just because you think you can do this doesn't mean you should. I'm not going to stand down and let you trample all over me and my town."

"Avery, you can't—"

"I *can* and I *will*," she cut in, glaring at him with a red-streaked face with blotches of mascara lingering at the corners of her glassy eyes. "Just watch me. Doesn't it bother you that you're hurting people when you make such major changes in their towns? You're not just knocking down one cabin to build a resort. You're knocking down businesses that have been here for decades. Family businesses. For some reason you are blind to the fact that individuals and families have their whole lives here. Marston Enterprises will change that, and I don't care what you say, it's not all good, or even mostly good. You want to come here and make major changes? Well, you can't. There are zoning laws."

"I'm aware of that. That's why I'm here."

"Well…well…" she stammered, obviously trying to come up with another threat that would work for her. "There's…"

He waited, but she didn't say more. Not surprising, really, since at the end of the day, there wasn't any legitimate way for her to fight him and his company.

The worst part was, he didn't want to hurt her. He'd never before come up against such a situation, where he felt personally involved with what was going on. He'd always landed in a small town, worked out the kinks in whatever laws the municipality might have against building a large resort and left without a hitch.

Sure, he'd spent time with some of the people, especially those on the town councils, but he'd never *felt* anything. And that was the problem now.

His emotions were going haywire.

Now he felt as if he was driving his Mustang too fast on one of those dirt roads so common around here, bumping all over the place and fishtailing like crazy, barely able to keep a hold of the steering wheel to keep from crashing. If only there was some way to solve Avery's problem and still do the job he'd been sent in to do.

But that was impossible.

Because it was personal. Avery hadn't even made it just about her bed-and-breakfast. Now she was defending the whole town of Whispering Pines.

*Her* town.

And he had a job to do—a job he was suddenly loath to do.

Suddenly Jake heard a couple of male voices along with the clunking sound of boots at the front door.

Avery glanced in that direction, appearing relieved at the sound. "Sharpe. Frost," she called, her voice cracking under the strain of her emotions. "In the kitchen."

Jake had seen Avery's brothers at church and around town a few times, but he'd only been briefly introduced to them once. He'd never really spoken to them. They seemed like nice enough guys, but when they entered the kitchen, their gazes quickly moved from their sister's glassy eyes and tear-streaked face to Jake, who was now standing on the opposite side of the counter.

Their expressions went from pleasant to angry and intimidating in a nanosecond.

Jake was a large man who worked out regularly, and not many men could threaten him, but Avery's brothers were likewise tall and muscular, and he had no doubt he'd be toast if they tried to take him two on one. If he didn't defuse this situation pronto he could be in real trouble here.

Frost, who had blond hair and compelling silver eyes that matched his name, moved around next to Jake, leaning his elbows on the counter and never taking his concerned gaze from Jake. Sharpe, a dark-haired man, narrowed his blue eyes on Jake, leaned his shoulder against the door frame and crossed his arms in an intimidating fashion.

"Avery? Sweetheart? Are you okay?" Frost asked in a deceptively mild tone. "What's going on?"

Avery glared at Jake, then scoffed and shook her head. "Nothing."

"Are you sure?" asked Sharpe. "This doesn't look like *nothing* to me. Is this guy giving you trouble? It looks as if you've been—"

"No worries," Avery cut in before Sharpe

could finish. "We're just busy making sandwiches for a picnic. Jake's mom and his daughter are down at the picnic area by the creek, and they're waiting for us. Nothing to see here."

"If you say so," said Frost, turning toward Jake. "You go ahead and finish making your sandwiches."

"Frost," Avery protested. "Leave it."

"But just so you know, *Jake*," said Sharpe, punching the air with his words, "we have our eyes on you."

"No kidding," Jake said under his breath. He could definitely feel their glares and the emphasis on his name was enough to make him tense his muscles.

"Please, guys," she protested. "You don't have to go all protective on me. I can handle my own problems."

"So, he is a problem, then." Sharpe stepped deeper into the room and stood on the opposite side of Jake, who was itching to walk away before things got really fired up. "If you hurt our sister, you'll answer to us."

It was good the way Sharpe and Frost took care of their sister. He appreciated the way

Avery's family closed ranks to protect her. He only wished it wasn't on him.

"No, that's not what I meant," Avery said, and then quickly changed the subject. "Can I make you guys a sandwich?"

"Yeah, of course. Like you even have to ask?" Frost said, grinning at his sister.

Jake breathed a silent sigh of relief, thankful that Avery was able to distract her brothers with food.

"Two for me," said Sharpe. "Loaded with everything."

When Avery met Jake's gaze, he could see she'd tucked her emotions away and was in total control again. Her face was expressionless, and somewhere along the way she'd wiped the tears and mascara blotches off her face. "Please finish making the lemonade, will you, Jake?"

"I… Sure thing," he said, thrown off by the way she'd been able to switch gears so rapidly. Her voice was, if not friendly, then at least calm.

He knew she was putting on a good show for her brothers, but he also knew this conversation wasn't over. As much as he admired Avery, or maybe because he recognized his attraction to Avery, the best course of action for him was to focus, get his work done in Whispering Pines and get out as fast as possible.

He hadn't felt this kind of chemistry with a woman since his wife's death. In all honesty, he'd thought he'd never feel such things again.

How could he?

The guilt was still there. It never left him, not for a second, digging into his gut at random times when he least expected it. Whenever he thought about his last moments with his pregnant wife Amber, how they'd been fighting, how he hadn't settled anything between them when he left for a business trip, it was almost more than he could bear.

He'd thought it might get better with time, but it hadn't.

There was no resolution to the problem because Amber was gone, and he couldn't tell her he was sorry.

For everything.

While he was walking away, getting in his car, driving to the airport, getting on the airplane, he'd known better.

*Don't let the sun go down on your anger.*

He'd not only done that, but he hadn't called her once in the week he was gone. Instead, he'd stewed silently in his anger alone in his hotel room.

And then he returned home believing everything would be fine and they would be able to just talk it out like they always did whenever they argued. Instead, he'd found her lying unconscious, having lost her balance somehow and landed with her head hitting the hard concrete, the annuals she'd intended to plant by the side of the walkway scattered around her.

He'd called 9-1-1. He had ridden in the back of the ambulance with her, holding her limp hand. He'd stayed by her bedside in the hospital for days as doctors worked hard to wake her from her coma.

She'd never opened her eyes again.

Through God's grace, Lottie had been safely born through cesarean section, but her epilepsy—

That was all on him.

He was certain Lottie's epilepsy was due to her mother being in a coma for so many days before the doctors had made the decision to deliver her via C-section. If only he had gotten home earlier…

After that tragedy, he never imagined another woman would make him feel again. What was happening between him and Avery, the sparks that exploded so ferociously whenever they clashed, was gut-wrenching and frightening in their intensity.

Which was yet another reason for him to tie things up here in Whispering Pines at the earliest possible moment and flee town as fast as he could.

Far, far away from Avery Winslow and the things she did to his mind and heart.

# Chapter Six

Avery unlatched the first of two gates and allowed everyone through into what was essentially a holding pen. She closed the first gate before opening the second one, which led into the petting zoo. The petting zoo was her sister Molly and her husband Logan's brainchild and was a big draw to the farm.

Landscaping customers often enjoyed visiting with the animals after they'd finished their shopping, but it wasn't as crowded this time of year as it was around Christmas, when everyone was looking for the perfect tree. In December, they kept all the animals out on a rotational basis, and the petting zoo was nearly always full of laughing children and curious parents.

The rest of the year, they kept a few animals out in the pen for prospective customers to visit, but today she'd asked Ruby and Frost to put all of them out so Lottie would have the full petting-zoo experience.

Frost was their main man where the farm animals were concerned. He had a matched pair of gray Percherons he used to give Saturday sleigh rides in the winter and hayrack rides in the summer. He also took care of everything in the barn and had happily let out all the animals.

Fortunately, he'd done that *before* he'd met up with Jake in the kitchen. Otherwise, he might not have been quite as willing to help.

Avery and Jake hadn't spoken much since their discussion—if it could be called that—in the kitchen. They'd brought the sandwiches, bags of chips and the pitcher of lemonade to the picnic area and enjoyed lunch together by the creek. It was a little cool and crisp, and they all had kept on their winter jackets as they ate, but it wasn't bad for the end of winter. Spring would soon be here, with green grass and colorful wildflowers peeking out from under the snow.

Winslow's Woodlands was a sight to behold year-round, and Avery was proud of the business her parents had created, and what she and her siblings had done with it since they'd grown up and brought their own work and ideas. And now with Molly and Logan's addition of the petting zoo, even visiting children were delighted no matter what time of year they came.

Avery and Jake had let Lottie do most of the talking as they ate. If Jake's mom noticed the wall of ice between the two of them, she didn't comment on it. Instead, she chatted on merrily with Lottie and directed the general conversation onto neutral ground.

Avery had suddenly found she wasn't too hungry and had quickly set her sandwich aside, choosing instead to nibble on a few chips and sip on her glass of lemonade.

As they entered the petting-zoo enclosure, Jake, who had Lottie's hand firmly in his, approached the feed machine, which doled out handfuls of grain pellets for a quarter. Avery had planned in advance and had a pocketful of quarters in her jeans for just this purpose. She took a couple out and helped Lottie and Elaine get their grain pellets.

Two black-and-white-spotted pygmy goats with curved horns bumped their way through the pack of mismatched animals to the front of the line, and Jake crouched next to Lottie to help her hold her grain pellets so one of the goats didn't steal them all away, which he appeared eager to do. The other goat nudged Jake's leg and bit at the denim of his jeans, pressing for a snack.

Jake laughed at the little goat's antics, and Lottie giggled.

"He's funny, Daddy," she said. "Can we feed him?"

Avery's heart clenched as she watched the domestic scene, Jake helping Lottie flatten her palm so the goat could nibble off it.

Lottie was so precious, giggling and squealing at the goat's lips on her hand. And watching Jake with her almost made Avery forget that they were on opposite sides of a very large fight.

She didn't know what was worse—knowing what Jake could be, or knowing who he could be. A cutthroat businessman, or a tender father.

For the first time since meeting Jake and his family, she considered the possibility of simply letting it all go, setting aside the cabin of her heart and finding somewhere else to create her bed-and-breakfast. And letting Marston Enterprises win the day and build their resort.

They were going to do it, anyway, weren't they?

And if she didn't fight them? What would happen then? What *could* happen?

Might she and Jake become friends? More than friends?

That was dangerous thinking, and she was going to nip it in the bud right now. Resort or no resort, bed-and-breakfast or not, fighting the big bad corporation or leaving it be, she could not and would not let herself fall for Jake Cutter.

She couldn't.

Two years ago, she'd been in a serious relationship with a local man, T.J.—or at least she'd thought it was serious. He was a single father with a six-year-old son. Their relationship hadn't lasted long, less than a year, and frankly she was happy to part ways with T.J. because they didn't have the same outlook on life. She soon discovered his Christian faith was only surface deep and she knew it would never work out between them in the long run.

Except that even in the short time they'd

been together, she'd spent a great deal of time with his son Oliver. And when she and T.J. broken up, she was no longer even allowed to see the boy.

Being parted from Oliver had been far more heartbreaking than splitting up her mediocre relationship with T.J.

And that was why, even if the other problems suddenly disappeared between her and Jake, she could never date him. The attraction she felt for Jake was far too powerful, and it would be far too easy to fall in love with Lottie—and she could even see how simple it would be to develop a close relationship with Elaine. She really liked the woman's easygoing personality.

No. It was better this way, staying at odds with Jake and letting him and his family leave as they planned.

Avery put in three more quarters and got some more of the grain pellets as the Cutter family moved through the petting zoo, feeding some of the animals and petting others. She'd seen plenty of happy families appreciating the animals, but she'd never enjoyed watching them quite as much as she did with the Cutters. Lottie exclaimed in delight over the sheep's thick wool and how soft Guapo the alpaca was, laughing when he nuzzled her hair with his long muzzle.

"*Guapo* means *handsome* in Spanish," Avery told them. "It fits this guy quite well, don't you think? He's an especially interesting animal. Alpacas are used both for their soft wool and as pack animals in Central and South America."

Not surprisingly, the pygmy goats were her constant companions no matter where they were in the enclosure, following all of them around and making a general nuisance of themselves.

"These little guys obviously love the grain pellets you're feeding them," Avery told the Cutters regarding the goats, "but they'll eat anything—and I do mean anything. We often let them graze around the farm to keep the grass down. Beats having to pull out a lawn-mower to get at the weeds."

Avery was surprised at how relaxed she was feeling, especially after the way she'd gone head-to-head with Jake in the kitchen earlier. Something about the fresh air and having the blessing of exposing a child to new experiences, especially with the animals she loved, had lifted both her heart and her attitude.

"I'll be right back," she said, leaving the petting zoo and heading for the barn. Since the Shetland pony was brand-new to the farm, Frost hadn't yet put him out in the pen.

But Avery had made a promise, and she knew the little pony would be the literal star of the show, at least to Lottie.

Shetlands could be mischievous creatures and weren't always reliable, which was why he wasn't allowed to wander with the other animals in the petting-zoo enclosure yet, especially because he was so new to the farm and would have to get used to enthusiastic children talking loudly and wanting to pet him.

"Hey, little guy," Avery said, approaching the pony and running a hand over his muzzle, smiling as she scratched the perfect white star on his forehead. "You're getting a name blessing today by the sweetest little girl you'll ever meet," she said. "What do you think about that?"

It took her less than a minute to halter the Shetland and bring him out to the waiting Cutter family.

"Here he is," Avery said, surprised at how much enthusiasm was surging through her at the thought of introducing the pony to the little girl. She had always loved giving gifts, especially to children, and this was a special one. "Hey, Lottie. I haven't told him the secret yet. Do you see his star here? You were the one who picked out his name, so do you want to be the one who gets to tell him what it is?"

Jake scooped the girl into his arms so she could run her fingers across the star on the Shetland's forehead.

"Your name is Star," Lottie pronounced, every bit as elegantly as if she were a princess christening a ship.

She really was a sweet little princess. Avery's heart warmed and swelled in her chest, and she had to swallow hard to keep her emotions under control.

"I think he likes it," Jake said as Star tossed his head and nickered.

"Can I ride him?" Lottie asked.

Jake and Elaine both turned inquiring gazes on Avery.

Avery realized she should have been prepared for that question, but she wasn't. Other than knowing Star was fairly young, Avery didn't know his background, since Frost had been the one who had purchased him. But Frost was an expert with horses and was a mature and responsible man, so she knew he would have gone out of his way to find a gentle animal who wouldn't easily spook to be part of the petting zoo.

"I think it would be okay if you want to set her on Star's back for a minute. Keep your arms around her waist, though, just in case Star shifts," Avery suggested, curling her fingers through Star's halter and holding his head firm.

"Yes, of course," Jake said. "Okay, Lottie, honey, here you go."

For a man who'd come straight from city life, he managed to put Lottie on Star without unsettling the Shetland even a little.

"Hold on to Star's mane, sweetheart," Avery said, slightly concerned when Lottie's excitement bubbled over into her hands and her legs started pumping.

"Easy, honey," Jake urged. "We don't want to scare the pony."

Actually, Star was performing magnificently, not appearing to be the least bit interested in the wiggling human on his back at all.

If only Avery could find the same peace in her heart while enjoying time with Jake and his family.

She could take a lesson from Star.

Despite the argument they'd had in the kitchen, Jake was enjoying his day out at the Winslow's Christmas-tree farm. He hadn't spent much time in the mountains, with its crisp, clean air laced with the pungent scent of evergreens, and he found he really liked it. He suspected a man could take a daily run through the wilderness trails and find true peace in the presence of God here.

There was so much to appreciate. The Lord's wonders were all around him, from the magnificent, towering boulders, which would be the envy of any sculptor, to the stunning lodge pines reaching for the sky and whispering in the wind. The aspen trees would be in full foliage in a couple of months, and Jake could only begin to imagine the golden hues of fall here at the farm.

It was an entirely different kind of existence than anything he'd known before, and he found himself a little envious of the Winslows' laid-back lifestyle. What he wouldn't give to slow down even for a little while and just be present for a change instead of always having to push forward and think ahead.

"Piggies," Lottie exclaimed, and Jake couldn't help but laugh along with Avery and his mom. Lottie had the attention span of—well, of a three-year-old little girl—and apparently she'd had enough of riding the pony for now.

He plucked her off the back of Star and set her on the ground next to the litter of wiggling pink piglets.

"Go ahead and enjoy the piggies while I get Star back into his stall," Avery suggested. "The piglets especially like to be scratched on their bellies. And they make really funny grunting sounds if you get just the right spot."

When she returned, she had a pretty, lingering smile on her face, and her expression was deep and thoughtful. Jake couldn't help the way his heart responded to her. She was just so beautiful, inside and out.

What man wouldn't look twice?

"We have a couple of other horses you'll have to meet sometime," Avery said, nodding toward the barn. "They are Frost's pride and joy, a matched pair of gray Percherons."

"Those are draft horses, right? Like Clydesdales?" Jake asked, attempting to display what little country knowledge he had. He'd actually taken Lottie to Denver's National Western Stock Show just before they'd arrived in Whispering Pines, and they had seen both types of draft horses pulling stagecoaches during the rodeo.

"Yes," Avery said, her eyes widening in surprise. "They're draft horses. I'm impressed that you know that."

Jake grinned and gave himself a mental pat on the back. Score one for him.

"Anyway, every Saturday afternoon year-round, Frost takes them out and offers our guests special rides—hayrack rides in the summer and sleigh rides in the winter. It's quite an enjoyable experience to bundle up underneath wool blankets and feel the cool air in your hair. You ought to try to get out here and take a ride before—that is—"

Avery stammered to a stop, her face reddening.

"That sounds great," said Elaine. "I know

Lottie would love to do that. And I'm totally up for it, too."

Jake didn't know whether his mom was just being polite or if she'd seen the sudden wall appear between Avery and Jake, but either way he quietly sighed in relief. He had so been enjoying this family outing and the time with Avery that, for a while, he'd almost forgotten he had to walk on eggshells around her.

"Do we need reservations?" he asked.

"When would you like to come?"

"A week from Saturday?"

"Perfect. I'll let Frost know. Be here at noon. He usually heads out about twelve thirty."

"I…uh… Super," he stammered, not quite sure what had just happened. One second Avery was pushing him away, and the next she was inviting him and his family back to her farm for another unique Winslow experience.

Maybe she was just being nice for Lottie's and his mom's sake. Maybe she didn't plan to be there a week from Saturday, and he wouldn't have to see her at all.

But maybe he wanted to.

# Chapter Seven

Avery unlocked the door to the Meyers' cabin and let herself inside, her heart beating a mile a minute as she walked over to the long, carved-oak dining room table, and flopped her computer bag down at the head of the table with a contented sigh. The oak could stand to have a good polish, and Avery made a mental note to add that to her ever-growing list of items she'd need to accomplish before opening the doors to guests for her bed-and-breakfast. These were her favorite kinds of tasks—ones involving elbow grease she'd be able to accomplish on her own.

There was no doubt in her mind—not that there ever was. But she was more convinced than ever, sitting here breathing in the ambiance that was this cabin. This was her dream house, the one she'd been searching for since the first day the idea of providing a bed-and-breakfast to A New Leash on Love clients had popped into her head. She knew this was her special place despite Marston Enterprises, and even after pushing back and forth with Jake over it—or maybe especially after they'd butted heads once again on the matter.

Every single thing about this cabin was perfect, from the roundabout porch to the industrial-fitted kitchen to the bright, cheery mother-in-law suite she could easily remodel. There was a perfect spot in the backyard where she planned to dig a nice vegetable garden. She'd get Sharpe, Frost and Ruby to build a play area for the kids, similar to the one they had at the farm.

Her brain was overflowing with ideas, and she couldn't pull her laptop out fast enough, turning it on and quickly navigating to a document which contained a spreadsheet with all her ideas. There was so much to do, and every single moment of work would be pure joy for her.

A cutthroat, get-the-job-done man such as Jake would never understand what it meant to just *feel* something was right the way she felt about this cabin. He took his orders from a big corporation and didn't ask questions. He was a figure-it-out and make-it-happen guy. She'd give him that much credit.

But she was equally determined to make it happen. And he wouldn't find it so easy to bulldoze through her dreams and goals as he might believe.

Much had happened since she'd seen him nearly a week ago. She'd spoken to the Meyers, for one thing, first, to get access to their house without always having to bother Lisa, and second, to find out if she was wasting her time going up against Marston. If they'd already done a deal, signed, sealed and delivered, then no amount of fighting would help.

As it turned out, the Meyers had just officially listed the property, and Avery was the only one who'd shown interest. The Meyers didn't even know who Marston Enterprises was.

Which meant what? That Jake was waiting to bring down the hammer? That the company was so sure of themselves they didn't even bother with preliminaries?

Avery knew enough to understand real-estate transactions didn't move quickly. There were hoops to jump through, everything from checking on zoning laws to going through property inspections and waiting for the Meyers to make any necessary changes before the sale could go through. In Avery's case, there was also the need to qualify for a mortgage in order to buy a house, but she'd thought ahead and had already prequalified.

She had the means to buy this house.

If Jake and his company didn't sweep it out from underneath her.

In addition to the Meyers, she'd also spoken to friends and neighbors around town to try to understand their perspectives on a Marston resort moving into the area. She knew how she felt about it, but it wasn't all about her. Even though in her heart she knew they were country people at heart like her, she still half expected more of them to be enthusiastic about the build.

Bringing in movie stars and other celebrities? That had to count for something, didn't it? People wanting to see their favorites face-to-face, maybe get an autograph or two?

But surprisingly, most of her neighbors didn't care for the idea of that much increased traffic in the area. Like Avery, they could see beyond the twinkling stars to the trouble such a resort could cause their small town.

She wasn't just fighting for herself.

She was fighting for them.

She was deep in the midst of searching for possible ways to stop Marston Enterprises in their tracks, when suddenly there were three loud thumps on the front door.

Avery was so startled by the sound she nearly jumped out of her skin. She'd come here for quiet and privacy, so she could think and plan out her strategy against Jake and Marston Enterprises. It was often noisy at home, even when she shut the door to her office.

Besides which, she wanted to draw in the ambiance of the place as she worked. The only one who even knew she was here was Felicity, and if there was a problem, her sister would have texted or called her on her cell phone, not come to the cabin.

Tentatively, she peeked out the front blinds to see Jake standing on the front porch, casually dressed in jeans and a royal blue button-down Western shirt with his usual black cowboy hat and boots. She knew without a closer glimpse that the color of his shirt would bring out the blue in his eyes.

The charming, sparkling eyes she would absolutely *not* get lost in today.

She opened the door so abruptly it clearly startled Jake, whose dark eyebrows rose for a moment before he recovered himself and swept off his hat.

"What do you want?" she demanded without a greeting.

"Well, hello to you, too."

She frowned at him.

"May I come in?" he asked in that honeyed Texas drawl as he nodded toward the inside.

"Why?"

Again, she'd clearly caught him off guard. "I…uh…"

She sighed, stopping just short of rolling her eyes as she stepped back out of the doorway and gestured for him to go by her. "Fine. Come in."

"Thank you."

"So…" she began, "what brings you to this neck of the woods?" She walked back to the dining-room table and seated herself at her laptop, assuming Jake would take the seat across from her.

Or rather, she hoped he would, as that would give her a modicum of distance from him.

Instead, he sat down next to her, blatantly checking out her handwritten notes and the site she was currently visiting on her computer screen.

Annoyed, she slammed her spiral notebook closed and minimized the screen on her laptop.

"Nosy much?" she groused.

He grinned back at her and shrugged. "More like curious."

"Well, you know what they say about curiosity and cats."

"Guess it's a good thing I'm not a cat."

"Aren't you?" He was like a panther, silently padding around her, ready to pounce on her dreams with his sharp claws out.

The corner of his lips tipped up in the heartwarming half smile that Avery could not resist reacting to no matter how hard she tried.

And she *was* trying.

"Fully domesticated house kitty," he said. "Couldn't hurt a mouse. You can ask my mom about that."

Avery snorted. Whatever else Jake Cutter was, it was *not* domesticated. She could sense a wild streak a mile long inside him. It was part of what made him so good at his work. That alpha-male, take-charge, get-the-job-done attitude.

"So, again, I ask, why are you here?" she pressed. He'd just suddenly happened to appear at the Meyers' cabin for no reason? She didn't believe that for a single, solitary second. "You wouldn't be following me, would you?"

He clasped his hand to his heart and gripped it as if she'd mortally injured him.

"What? Me? Never!" He then paused to think about what he'd just said. "Not that you're not eminently worthy of following."

"Do you ever speak without using that smooth tongue of yours?"

He combed his hair back with the palm of his hand as his grin widened. "I can't help it. I was born smooth."

She could believe that. In high school he'd probably been voted Most Popular, along with Most Likely to Succeed and undoubtedly Class Clown.

"So, if you're not following me, how did you know I was here?"

"Oh, I didn't. Not at first, anyway, until I saw your SUV parked up next to the house. Despite your entrancing nature, I wasn't actually looking for you. I stopped by to walk the woods a bit, check the land out and make some notations for Marston. I'm enjoying the mild weather and the fresh air, and the truth is I like hiking through the woods. You just don't get that in Dallas."

"Is that where you live? Dallas?"

"At the moment, yes. That's where Marston has its home offices. I have an apartment there where my mother and I currently live with Lottie—not that we're there much. But spending time in a little town like Whispering Pines tempts me to make a major move. There is definitely something to be said for raising a child in such a wonderful environment."

"Jake," Avery protested, "do you even hear what you're saying?"

He folded his hands on the table and leaned toward her. "Why don't you tell me?"

"You already know. A Marston resort is going to change everything about this town. You'll be putting pressure on the small-town businesses. Many won't survive in the new landscape you're proposing."

"Maybe. But there will be all kinds of new opportunities. The resort will provide lots of new jobs."

"And all of those people who want to take those jobs—where are they all going to live? What's it going to do our town?"

"So, you grow. Expand."

"Maybe we don't want that. If you did move to Whispering Pines, it may very well turn into a town like Aspen. The kind of place where you can't take your child into any of the stores because everything is flashy and expensive. Compare that to what we have now—stores where Lottie can go in and find stuffed animals and T-shirts placed at eye level."

She leaned back and crossed her arms with a huff. "That's the difference, the real difference. And that's what I'm talking about. Are you really ready to be responsible for ruining Whispering Pines ?"

Avery had a point, and it was razor-sharp. Plus, she had no qualms about jabbing him with it over and over again.

Did she truly think he didn't have a heart?

Well, he did, and he was seriously considering what she had said.

Maybe she was right. But at this point, there wasn't much he could do about it. He had a job to do, and that job was to secure the Meyers' property for Marston Enterprises. It didn't matter how he personally felt about the matter.

He couldn't just quit his stable, well-paying job because he suddenly didn't like what he was doing. He had to provide for his daughter and his mother. Lottie had serious medical issues that required medicines and treatments that weren't cheap, and he would always seek out the very best in care for her. Eventually she'd want to go to college, and he wanted to be prepared for that, too. His daughter was so smart he was sure she'd be able to get into any Ivy League school she wanted. Of course, she was only three years old right now, but he knew that she had an amazingly bright future ahead of her.

And that future required having a lot of money in savings and investments. He'd worked hard to get where he was at Marston over the past six years. He'd been telling the truth when he'd said to Avery that he wouldn't mind raising Lottie in a small town such as Whispering Pines. It just wasn't practical. Not for him.

It would never happen.

She was making too much sense with what she was saying, and she was getting to him. He felt the sudden urge to put some emotional space between them.

"So, your notebook and laptop there. Did you come by the Meyers' place to find some peace and quiet away from the farm?" he asked.

She stared at him silently for a moment, probably wondering at the sudden change of subject.

"Yes," she said after a long while.

"Business?"

"You could say that. I'm making plans for my bed-and-breakfast."

He felt as if she'd gut-punched him, and the worst part was, he'd walked right into it. He should've been ready for that answer.

"It's easier for me to picture the changes I need to make if I'm right here in the middle of all this," she continued. "Walking through the house gives me such a sense of excitement and anticipation."

"Avery…" he said tenderly.

"I don't want to hear it." She blew out a breath. "Jake, we've already traveled this road. Repeatedly. You do your thing. I'll do mine."

"Yes, but—"

"I've been doing some interesting research," she said, interrupting him.

"Oh, yeah? What about?"

"Are you aware there are several plants and animals on the endangered-species list that are indigenous to this region?"

He hadn't known that. It hadn't even occurred to him, as no one had ever brought it up in prior deals.

"It's quite fascinating reading, really. It's important that we don't build in areas where these plants and animals live. I've just scratched the surface so far and have no idea just how many there are altogether. It's really opened my eyes to all of God's creations."

"Are you trying to tell me I'm going to have difficulties when I try to get the zoning laws changed for the resort area?"

She shrugged and didn't quite meet his

gaze. "I'm not trying to tell you anything. You asked me what I was doing here. That's what I'm doing."

She was going to use what she'd discovered against him. She wasn't going to back down no matter what he said. He knew that now. If she had to fight a huge corporation who could smash her under their heel, she would. If she had to face Goliath with a mere sling and a stone, that's exactly what she would do.

It wasn't that he was in any way concerned she would succeed in her endeavors. He didn't find that humorous or her stubbornness annoying, although he might as well, as she was getting in the way of what he needed to do to finish his job here.

Instead, with Avery, he admired her strength of spirit and singlemindedness.

She didn't want this house for her own benefit but to minister to others. If it was solely up to Jake, he'd let her have it and look elsewhere for the resort.

She'd changed some things for him. He realized whether or not they built the resort here or in another small town, many of Avery's concerns were the same no matter where he went. Six of one and half a dozen of the other. He'd been smashing into small towns and changing them, for better or worse, since he'd started doing this job.

It gave him a lot to think about.

"I don't want to argue with you anymore," he admitted softly, reaching out and taking her hand.

She glanced down at where their hands met, but to his surprise, she didn't snatch hers away as he'd expected her to do. "Neither do I."

"Even if we're on opposite sides?" he asked in a whisper.

"Even then. Maybe especially then."

"Good." He hadn't expected it to be that easy for them to come to an understanding. He captured her gaze and saw the same astonishment registered there. She was no less surprised than he was.

"Good," she echoed.

He wanted to mark this change in their relationship with something tangible, but putting a boulder in the yard to signify their cease-fire didn't seem quite right for the occasion. Maybe something a little more fun.

"Tomorrow is Friday," he stated, as if that

was some important information of which only he was aware.

"Yes, it is," she agreed, a small smile creeping onto her lips.

"Lottie," he continued. He paused but Avery didn't interrupt him. "She likes to ice-skate. I hear the outdoor rink at Winslow's Woodlands is open on Friday nights."

"It is, at least for a few more weeks, while the ice is still nice and solid."

"Do you—I mean, are you going to be there?"

"I don't make it a habit of attending the Friday-night skates. Not recently, anyway. I used to love to ice-skate when I was a kid, but things have gotten very busy lately."

He swallowed hard, knowing she had purposefully stopped just short of saying *why* she was so busy.

But this was important, and he hoped Avery would see that. Lottie had started lessons this year, and with the grace of a small child had picked it up right away. Jake had never been on the ice in his life. So, his next words were hazardous in more ways than one.

"Would you make an exception for tomor-

row night?" he asked and then tunneled on-
ward before he could talk himself out of it.
"I'm planning to take my mom and Lottie
out to the rink, and I know they would both
love to see you."

Avery glanced down at her notebook and
then back up at him. "To be honest, I've
spent so much time planning for my bed-and-
breakfast that I'm behind in my paperwork
for the farm and service-dog rescue. I was
planning on using Friday night to catch up."
She pinched her lips for a moment. "But…"

She paused and looked down at their fingers, which were still touching.

"But?" he asked, his breath catching in his
throat as he waited for her answer.

"But I guess I can make an exception this
one time. Like I said, it's been a while since
I've gone skating, and I can use the exercise.
It sounds like fun." She looked up into his
eyes, and he thought he saw something soften
in them. "I'll see you tomorrow night, then?"

"Tomorrow night it is." He released her
hand, stood and replaced his black Stetson
on his head, tipping his hat to her as he did.
"I'll get out of your hair now so you can—"
he stopped and gestured toward her laptop

"—do whatever it is you need to do. Until tomorrow, then."

"Yes," she agreed, her voice soft and silky, making his stomach flutter with butterflies. "Until tomorrow."

# Chapter Eight

Avery's own voice silently mocked her in her mind. *I guess I can make an exception. I can use the exercise.*

She was an idiot. She'd had the perfect excuse to avoid spending time with him, and she'd capitulated faster than she could have said, *Lickety-split.*

Or even better and more to the point, *No, thank you.*

Why she'd agreed to go skating with the Cutter family was still a mystery. Of course, she genuinely enjoyed spending time with Lottie and Elaine, but that wasn't all it was, and she knew it.

She couldn't even hoodwink her sisters into believing this was all about a curly-haired three-year-old little girl, no matter how adorable Lottie was. They'd been teasing her nonstop about her date with Jake and his family ever since she'd made the mistake of mentioning it at breakfast Friday morning.

*She* hadn't used the word *date*, of course. She hadn't even *thought* the word *date*. They were all just meeting up to ice-skate, and it had nothing whatsoever to do with her growing attraction to Jake.

Right?

She supposed it had been so long since that she'd had an actual date that it wasn't at all surprising that her sisters would misconstrue what was happening—or not happening—between her and Jake.

Her brothers had also had a few words about the outing. If they had their way, none of their sisters would date any man ever. In their minds, no man would ever be good enough for any of the Winslow sisters. Every single time a man tried to date one of the Winslow girls, they were interrogated like hardened criminals and threatened with bodily harm.

Avery was just biding her time for the perfect woman to come along for each of her brothers so she would have her opportunity to pepper their dates with endless questions.

In the meantime, there was this date-that-wasn't-a-date happening this evening, which she now couldn't avoid. She dressed in jeans and a thick white cable-knit sweater, pulled on her snow boots and arranged a knit Broncos hat over her shoulder-length blond hair. She didn't bother to apply much makeup, other than a quick dab of mascara and some lip gloss. The crisp evening air would give her cheeks a nice pink glow. Being around Jake would be yet another reason for her cheeks to warm sans makeup.

After pulling on orange Broncos gloves that matched her hat, she picked up her white skates, their laces already neatly tied together, and slung them over her shoulder. The lake, secluded by the surrounding woodlands but well-lit with twinkling fairy lights Sharpe had installed ages ago, was on the northern border of the Winslow property and was within walking distance of the main house.

The rink was a town favorite, and they often had friends and neighbors over to skate on mild Friday evenings. It was one area of their business that they didn't charge for use.

Avery couldn't imagine asking her friends for money to share in what God had created. It was a blessing just to see everyone enjoying a family night out now and again.

In the summertime, they made up for not charging for the lake's use in winter. They outfitted the lake with rainbow trout, which was a special treat especially for local children on summer break from school. Trout were easy to catch and made a nice dinner for the family back home, as well as offering the kids a point of pride when their lines jerked tight and their bobbers dunked under the surface.

She let her sister Felicity, who was watching television curled on the couch with a roaring fire in the fireplace and three dogs curled around her, know she was on her way to the rink.

Avery quietly snorted and shook her head as she stepped out into the cool evening, adjusting her scarf around her neck as she walked. Despite the chill, it was a lovely evening. At the farm, she was able to see millions of twinkling stars above her, and on the darkest, moonless nights, even the thick, cloudy rainbow of the Milky Way stretching across the sky. Tonight the moon was nearly full, lending its beam of light to her path, although she also carried a flashlight with her so she didn't accidentally stumble on a rock or an errant tree root. She knew the path she was walking like the back of her hand, but having lived on this mountain all her life, she also knew better than to take any unnecessary chances. There was always the possibility of running into wildlife.

She loved what she and her family were doing with their business. Every year one of the siblings thought of something new and exciting to add to the farm to make it more well-rounded for their customers, especially the kids, and Avery was stoked to see how it grew from there. All of the Winslow siblings were creative in their own ways, which was what made their business such a hit, and not only in Whispering Pines. Customers drove in from as far as Denver and Colorado Springs to spend a day enjoying themselves here.

But right now, her mind wasn't on business so much as how she was going to make it through the coming evening with Jake. She was more nervous than excited. At least she knew how to ice-skate, so that was one less thing to worry about. She'd taken lessons for several years as a child and could still do a pretty decent double axel.

She spotted Jake the moment she arrived at the lake. He was still at his car helping Lottie out of the back seat of his red Mustang. He then hung child-size pink ice skates over his broad shoulder. Then he ducked back into the car and retrieved a large shoe box, which Avery guessed contained his ice skates. Elaine moved around the car to join her family, carrying her own skates.

"Jake," Avery called from a bench on the edge of the lake. He looked in her direction, and she waved. "Over here."

Sharpe had built benches around the lake with solid pine tree trunks sawed in half and carefully sanded so no one received unexpected slivers. They gave the area an old-fashioned feel, especially with the twinkling fairy lights draped around the perimeter.

Frost had backed up his truck to the edge of the rink and was blasting upbeat music from his large Bluetooth speaker set in the bed of the truck.

It felt—romantic.

*Dangerous*.

Her mind chimed with warning bells. It would be easy to succumb to the ambiance, especially with a handsome man like Jake around. But she wasn't going to do it. She was on her guard. Her defenses were mounted.

Besides, it wasn't as if she was alone with Jake. He had his family with him. She'd be skating with Lottie, too.

Which was perilous in its own way, but only if she let it be so. She just couldn't let herself become too attached to Lottie and Elaine. Awareness was everything. As long as she stayed aware of what she was doing and how she was feeling, she would be okay.

And there was a good-size group gathering to skate. It wasn't just her and the Cutters. That was yet another way to guard her heart.

Holding Lottie's hand, Jake and his mother walked over to the bench Avery had reserved for them.

"Hey," he said, greeting her with a hug around her shoulders which she immediately pulled away from. He probably didn't mean anything by it, being the naturally charming guy he was, but he was too friendly for his own good. It wasn't his fault her heart roared to life every time he touched her.

"We'd better get our skates on and get out onto the ice before it gets too crowded. I never know how many of our friends and neighbors may show up on any given night. Sometimes there's next to no one, but since there won't be too many more weeks of winter left, I expect lots of folks will come out to enjoy one of the last skates of the season." She took in a deep breath because she was completely out of air. "How long has it been since you've been on the ice?"

Avery was speaking a great deal faster than usual, a sure sign of how nervous she was. Hopefully Jake and his family didn't notice.

Jake chuckled and made a face. "The last time I've been on the ice? That would be today. I almost slipped on a patch of black ice coming out of the cabin we're renting— which reminds me that I need to salt that area when I get home, before our mail carrier slips on it."

Avery had the feeling Jake was likewise speaking a little too quickly and was offering up way too much information, just as she'd done a moment ago. Was it possible he was having some of the same feelings?

"The last time I've been on the ice with skates on?" Jake continued. "It depends on who you ask. My mom takes Lottie to lessons once a week. She started begging to learn how from the very first time she watched figure skating on television. Mom is quite the skater in her own right. She's been skating her whole life. As for me…" He held up the large box he'd tucked under his arm. "I just purchased these earlier today from Johnson's Sporting Goods."

"You're breaking in a new pair of skates tonight?" Avery asked, wondering if he realized his feet were probably going to be very sore afterward. "Did you work the leather or anything before you came, or use the heater to warm them up, at least?"

"Um—no. Was I supposed to?"

"Only if you don't want to feel as if your feet are falling off before the end of the evening. New leather isn't very pliable. Why'd you have to buy a new pair?"

"Uh…"

"He doesn't skate," Elaine cheerfully chimed in. "Never has."

"You don't skate?" Avery was stunned, and it showed clearly on her face. "But you were the one who—"

"Asked you to go skating with us. Yes, I know. And now I feel foolish, let me tell you. It was one of those brilliant spur-of-the-moment ideas. I had originally intended to bring Mom and Lottie and just sit here watching them skate."

"But of course now he wants to skate with you," Elaine said cheerfully. "He's hoping you can teach him how and give him a few pointers."

"Mom," Jake groaned, his face reddening above his beard.

"I can do that." Avery grinned. She hadn't had many opportunities where she had anything legitimate up on Jake since they'd met. She always felt as if she was scrambling to keep up with him. For once, the proverbial ball was in her court.

Or skates, as the case may be.

This could turn out to be a fun evening, after all.

Jake ignored his mother and dug the black skates from the box. If he hadn't been totally unsure about this before, he was completely unsure of it now. The man at the sporting-goods store had insisted he purchase a pair of skates that was a size smaller than his usual size and suggested he wear thick wool socks with them.

That seemed backward to Jake and made no sense whatsoever. If anything, he ought to have got a larger size if he was going to be wearing thick wool socks. But Mr. Johnson had insisted, so here he was.

And now Avery was reminding him about not having worked the leather, which he should have known about even if Mr. Johnson hadn't mentioned it when he was making the sale. Of course new leather would be stiff and unpliable.

Almost as stiff as he would be out on the ice.

"No walls?" he said, not even realizing he'd spoken aloud until he caught Avery's dumbfounded stare.

"It's a *lake*," she said, sounding as if she was speaking to a first grader.

Well, duh. Of course they wouldn't have a wall around a lake. It was just that he'd been picturing Lottie's indoor rink, which was also used by local hockey teams for practice and games. He'd been assuming he could hold on to the wall and slowly but surely make his way around the rink one small step at a time.

And now he was deeply regretting having invited Avery to join them. Why was he only now realizing that even had there been a wall, he was going to look like an uncoordinated dweeb on the ice. His sport was baseball, and he was quite good at it.

Hockey? Not so much.

He suspected he was going to spend most of his evening on his hands and knees. There wasn't even a fence surrounding Winslow's lake. Just open ice for him to repeatedly fall down on and make a total fool of himself.

"Of course," Jake answered belatedly, attempting to shove his feet into his very tight, unforgiving skates. "I knew there wouldn't be a wall. I was just kidding when I said that."

"Lace your boots up tight but not too tight," Avery offered. "You want the skates to feel secure around your feet but not pinch your toes."

It was far too late for that. They were already pinching, and he hadn't even stood up yet. Once he put his weight on them, they were going to downright hurt.

Avery had her skates on well before Jake managed to get both of his on and laced up, and when he glanced over at his mom and Lottie, he realized they, too, were waiting for him.

"Maybe you guys should—" he started, intending to suggest they go on without him. But when Avery raised her eyebrows, he let his sentence drop.

"Elaine and Lottie, go ahead and get out on the ice. I'll help Daddy make his way out there."

"Okay, I'll admit I may need a little help." He stood and wavered as he attempted to find his balance, but it wasn't as easy as he'd hoped. Standing on these little slivers of steel on the ground was incredibly difficult, and he wasn't even on the ice yet. What kind of horrible person had come up with the idea of using blades to get across the ice, anyway?

Avery held out her hand to him. "Come on. You can lean on me. It's actually easier to balance on your skates once you're on the ice."

He didn't believe her. Not for one moment. But he followed her, one painful, wobbly step after the other. His ankles were already screaming at him. When they reached the edge of the lake, Avery hopped onto the ice with both feet and skated out a bit, performing a graceful pirouette before returning to his side, holding both arms out in front of her and gesturing for him to hold on to her.

"Trust me. I'm here for you. Grab on to my forearms," she instructed, "and then just step out onto the ice as if you were walking."

He tried to do what she'd instructed. He really did. But the second the blade hit the ice, his foot slid forward. He attempted to balance with his other foot, but once both skates were on the ice, his legs went in very different directions than he'd intended, and his feet flew out from under him.

He was so focused on his feet that he didn't even think about the fact that he was grasping on to Avery for dear life—that is, until he was sprawled backward on the ice with Avery's head on his chest, her face muffled in his coat and her shoulders shaking.

How bad was she hurt?

Was that why she was crying?

"I'm so sorry," he said. "Don't move. Stay

right where you are. You may have injured your neck. Someone will call 9-1-1."

She rolled over onto one elbow on the ice and stared down at him. She had tears in her eyes and her shoulders were still shaking, but now Jake could see her shaking shoulders were caused by laughter.

"I doubt anyone noticed us fall down like that."

"You aren't hurt?"

She shook her head. "No, of course not. Are you?"

"Only my pride. I can't believe I knocked you over like that."

"No worries. It isn't the first time I've fallen on the ice, nor will it be my last. Kind of goes with the territory. Even Olympic skaters take diggers now and again."

His lips twitched with mirth. "I'll keep that in mind."

She easily rose to her feet, balancing on her skates as if it was nothing. "Are you able to get up?"

"I think so."

She reached her hand for him, but he ignored it, knowing that way led to another major *digger*, as she'd called it. He wasn't going to pull her back down if he could help it. Instead, he rolled to his hands and knees and carefully rose to his feet.

Lottie skated up to him and circled around him, laughing.

"Daddy, you fell down."

"Yes, sweetie, I did. I'm not very good at skating. Can you show me how you do it?"

The next half hour was spent with Jake gaining ice-skating instructions all around. Lottie liked to show rather than tell, and she was easily bored at having to stay with Daddy all the time, so she would skate around the rink and eventually return to his side, with his mother watching her to make sure she didn't run into any trouble. He sent up a quick prayer to God, grateful as always for his mother's help. He didn't know what he would do without her.

Unlike Lottie, Avery stayed right by his side. She was especially beautiful tonight, with the crisp air giving her cheeks a pretty blush and the light breeze flipping the edges of her hair as she skated. She appeared to be a big Broncos fan. It wasn't the first time he'd seen her decked out in fan gear. It was in her favor that she looked so good in orange.

He was well aware she could be off skating around the rink at least ten times around for every one lap of his, but she patiently taught him the basics of staying on one's feet while skating.

He did fall, but after the first time it wasn't as often as he'd anticipated, and usually it was because his mind accidentally wandered to thinking about the woman beside him instead of what he was supposed to be concentrating on, which was staying on his feet as his blades slid over the ice.

He might be slow, but not having a wall to lean on actually worked in his favor because he had to learn to balance on his own without a crutch. Avery was great with her encouragement. She told him to bend his knees, tuck when he fell so he didn't hurt himself or trip up other skaters, and use his arms to help keep him steady. He expected he might have been better off if he'd used wrist guards and knee pads, but the minor scrapes he incurred weren't going to hurt as bad as his feet tomorrow morning.

"Think you've got it?" Avery asked after an extended training session where she'd been unbelievably patient with him.

He grinned. "I've got the basics down. Enough to stay on my feet, anyway—most of the time."

"Do you mind if I take one quick turn around the rink on my own?"

He could see she was itching to do some real skating. "Please do. I've been hogging all of your skating time. I don't want you to feel as if I'm holding you back. You must be bored out of your wits having to skate so slowly with me."

She returned his smile, a sparkle in her blue eyes. "You're not holding me back. It's nice to feel useful."

For once there was no tension between them—and he was totally enjoying that. It was as if all the other problems had gone away, dissipating into the night and leaving only pleasure and happiness.

As he glanced around, he saw people— from little kids to older folks—glorying in mountain life under the twinkling fairy lights. His mom and Lottie were laughing together and having a blast holding each other's hands and twirling around.

He could seriously get used to this.

He watched as Avery skated away from

him, and it was only then that he realized the kind of control she had over the ice. She skated forward, then backward, then forward again, with her arms held out as gracefully as a professional dancer's. She gained speed, and the next thing he knew she was in the air, twirling once, and then twice, before her blades once more touched the ice.

He knew he was gaping, but he couldn't help it.

"That's called a double axel," said his mom from behind him, startling him. He hadn't even realized she'd skated to his side.

"That's amazing," he countered.

"It sure is. Not too many people can do that, especially as well as Avery just did. There was a time in my youth when I was able to do a single axel, but that was a long, long time ago. If Lottie keeps up with her lessons, you'll probably be seeing her doing double axels someday soon."

"Are you having fun, Lottie?" he asked, touching his daughter's shoulder. "I saw you out there twirling around with Grandma."

"The ice is so pretty," Lottie said, but her gaze was wandering to where Ruby was sitting on a bench with Sissy lying at her feet.

"I think we're going to take a little break," his mom said. "We're getting a bit tired out here. Anyway, Ruby brought hot cocoa and has Sissy along with her. Lottie wants to go say hi to the dog."

Jake counted on his mother to know when Lottie had had enough of something. He still wasn't great at reading the signs, and Lottie would get cranky if she became overtired.

"Mom?" he said, catching her elbow as she started to skate away.

She turned back with an inquisitive smile on her face.

"Thank you."

"No need, honey. You know I love you and Lottie more than anything. There's nowhere else I'd rather be than with the two of you."

"Still. I couldn't do it without you. I'd be totally lost."

She reached up and patted his scruffy cheek. "I know, son. I know."

Jake was just circling around the ice to find Avery when the music turned from upbeat pop music to a slow eighties ballad. Frost picked up a microphone attached to his sound system. It squeaked with feedback for a mo-

ment, and he laughed as he drew the microphone farther away from his lips.

"Time to find that special someone and
slow things down," he announced cheerily.
"Grab your partner. Couples only for this
skate."

Avery skated up beside him and skidded
to a halt, causing a cloud of shaved ice to fly
into the air.

She looked invigorated. Happy.

And as beautiful as he'd ever seen her. His
throat closed around his words.

"My mom said Ruby brought some hot
cocoa," he explained. His words were husky,
and his tone had dropped an octave. "She and
Lottie are over there with her now."

Avery glanced in the direction he indicated. "Oh, good. She brought Sissy along
like I asked her to. I'd really like Lottie to
get to know Sissy better."

Avery slipped her arm through his arm and
started slowly skating around the rink. He,
in turn, put his other hand on hers for balance and because it was a couples' skate and
that's what everyone else was doing—skating arm-in-arm or holding hands.

Seeing as it was a couples' skate, he'd assumed she'd want to sit this one out. He had intended to ask if she wanted some hot cocoa and had given her an opening to get off the ice, so he was surprised when she'd grabbed his arm so casually.

"You think Sissy would be good for Lottie?" he asked, feeling the need to talk to keep from focusing on the fact that he was hyperaware of her nearness, her arm linked with his, and the floral scent that was uniquely hers wafting around him, making him dizzy.

Romance was definitely in the air. He was feeling it with every beat of his heart. And for once, his brain wasn't arguing, wasn't bringing up the past to flaunt it in his face.

Tonight, it was just him and Avery. Together.

# Chapter Nine

Avery gracefully swirled around so she was facing Jake, then started skating backward, wrapping her arms around his neck. He placed his hands around her waist. They were able to make eye contact now, and their gazes were tightly locked, lost in each other's worlds.

For a minute, neither of them said a word.

"I absolutely think Sissy will be a wonderful service dog for Lottie," Avery said, finally breaking the silence and continuing the conversation from before. "Ever since we met at Sally's Pizza and I watched Sissy with Lottie when she was having her episode, I've been working with her every day to get her more comfortable with what an epileptic seizure looks and feels like and what she should do when it happens. Of course, as you saw that day, Sissy instinctively recognized the signs and alerted us to what was happening even before we could see anything was wrong—I believe Sissy knew what was going to happen even before Lottie felt she was going to seize. That's the amazing thing about dogs. They have a sixth sense we humans lack."

Avery took a breath. She was babbling again.

She'd never in her life said so many words in one go. Everything she was saying was important, and it was something she'd wanted to bring up to him at some point in the near future, but during the couples' skate at the lake was hardly the appropriate time to have such a conversation—or really, any conversation at all.

The truth was, she was reveling in how right it felt to be with Jake, his strong arms clasped firmly around her waist, his crisp masculine scent swirling through her senses.

She hadn't felt this way about a man in… well, maybe never, and the strength of these feelings frightened her. In mere weeks, she'd be opposing him at the town council meeting, fighting for the Meyers' land and the small-town way of life for Whispering Pines. And even if God somehow worked everything out in her favor, when it was all said and done, Jake and his family would be leaving.

That was his job, she knew, moving from one town to the next to build resorts for Marston Enterprises. He lived in a fancy Dallas apartment with a car valet and a doorman. No matter what feelings were developing between them, their lives were just too different.

Whether or not she succeeded in winning the Meyers' cabin, her life was here in Whispering Pines, working with her family to run a successful business and service-dog program.

So, even if Marston Enterprises took its business elsewhere, there could never be a Jake and Avery.

Jake stared deeply into her eyes.

"Penny for your thoughts?" he whispered, then lost his balance and had to stand straight again. He flashed an apologetic half smile.

"That's the problem with you city boys," Avery teased. "You try to intimidate people into giving you way more back than what you give to them."

His gaze widened in shock, and she wasn't

certain he realized she'd just been kidding around with him.

"Okay, for one thing, I'm thirty-six years old. That hardly qualifies as a boy. And second, I'm well aware your thoughts are worth far more than I could ever pay. But I promise to make that penny extra shiny."

Somehow, he'd made that last part sound romantic, and Avery swallowed hard, trying to regain her wits about her. How easy it would be to forget all the complications between them and just let everything go.

"It was just that your gaze became distant there for a moment," he explained. "And I wondered why."

There was no way Avery was going to admit what she was *really* thinking about, so she diverted his attention to a more pleasant subject.

Or at least a safer one.

"I was just thinking about you and me skating around like this. I don't get out here as often as I'd like, especially just to enjoy going around the rink with others. Mostly it's Frost and Ruby who keep things running out here. I pretty much stay in my office. I'm more of a spreadsheets-and-paperwork kind of girl."

"Woman," he whispered with a wink.

"Twice corrected, and true on both counts." He was right—he was very much a man and not a boy. The only boyish thing about him was his charm. And she'd lost her girlish ways long ago. As the oldest sibling, she'd kind of taken over after their parents had passed on.

"This kind of feels like a high-school dance. Haven't done any slow dancing in a while. Not that I'm complaining."

"It does, doesn't it? Except look around you. We've got everyone from junior-high kids to folks who have been married for fifty years."

"In some ways that makes it even more romantic," he whispered into her ear.

There weren't that many men who would consider it that way, and Avery had to admit she was impressed, especially when Lottie skated back out on the ice and scooched between Avery and her daddy.

"What's up, honey?" he asked with a grin.

"I want to skate with you and Miss Avery, Daddy."

"Of course, sweetie," Avery said, her heart welling. With a smile, she turned and took one of Lottie's hands while Jake took the other one. Together, the three of them finished off the couples' skate.

As much as Avery fought against it, she knew she was losing ground.

And fast.

If she wasn't careful, she was going to make the same mistake that she had made last time—falling in love with a man with a child. She didn't think she could handle that kind of heartbreak again.

A smart woman would make excuses. Walk away. Never look back.

And yet she skated on, hand in hand with Lottie and Jake.

Jake groaned as he unlaced his skates and pulled them off his aching feet, wiggling his toes to see if they were still attached and had any movement. Once he'd been out on the ice with Avery and his family, he'd given very little thought to the way his stiff skates didn't have the give they needed.

But he was paying for it now.

Avery had already removed her skates and put her snow boots on, so she walked over to where Jake was bent over his second foot, which still had a skate on it.

"Are you okay?" she asked, grabbing his heel and yanking at the skate to help him get it off.

"Ow," he answered, screwing up his face in a knot. "Just *ow.*"

"I will refrain from telling you 'I told you so,' mostly because I really enjoyed this evening and I'm glad you and your family came out to skate. Thank you for inviting me."

"It was worth it," he agreed, tugging on his snow boots with a sigh as he reveled in the comfortable plush inside.

"When you get home, put some warm water in the tub and soak your feet in Epsom salts. It'll help a little with the pain and swelling."

"Yeah, I will," he agreed. "Can I walk you to your car?"

"Oh, I didn't drive. It's only a short distance back to the house, and I enjoy walking in the fresh night air."

"Even in the dark? Isn't that a little dangerous?"

"Could be," she agreed. "But I know the path very well. I've been hiking it all my life."

"What about bears or mountain lions?" he asked, only half teasing.

"Well, I suppose there's the occasional lynx. And bears, sometimes. We have brown bears and the occasional grizzly. They can be a real nuisance with the trash cans."

"You are *so* not walking home alone, Ms. Winslow."

"Well, Mr. Cutter, I've been walking alone in the dark for years. I've got a nice, strong flashlight to help me see the path, and I know to make a lot of noise as I walk. Most wildlife will run away when they hear a sound they don't recognize."

"Maybe. But even without sharp-toothed tigers lingering in the area, my mama taught me manners. If I dance—uh, skate—with a woman, I walk her home."

Avery might be stubborn, but Jake could and would hold his own.

"What about your own family? Don't they need to get home?"

"Hold on a sec," he said when he noticed Frost packing up his sound system into the back of his truck.

"Hey, Frost," he called.

Frost met his gaze and raised his eyebrows

expectantly. His smile was slightly suspicious, and Jake knew his next words were only going to make it worse, but it wasn't as if he could blame Frost for wanting to protect his sister. Jake would feel the same if he had a sister. He just needed to prove to Frost that they were on the same page where Avery was concerned.

Jake likewise wanted to protect Avery—from everything about to go down with Marston Enterprises, for one thing.

She had a tender heart. It was part of what drew him to her.

He was well aware he could hurt her—in more ways than one.

"I'm going to have my mom drive Lottie back to our rental cabin in my car and then walk Avery home. Otherwise she'll be walking home alone, and I don't want her to do that. Would it be possible for you to meet us back at your house and give me a ride back to my place?"

Frost stared at him for a moment without speaking. Jake couldn't read his expression.

"Did you run this by Avery?" Frost asked doubtfully. "She's been hiking around in these woods for her whole life. It's not as if she needs an escort or anything."

"No, I know," Jake said. "I don't intend to wrestle any bears or anything. I just wanted to talk more to Avery about the service-dog Sissy. She really helped Lottie during a seizure, and Avery thinks she might be a good service animal for her."

Frost didn't look convinced. "So, you intend to have a serious conversation at the end of a romantic evening?"

Jake took a step back. "Romantic? Who said anything about romance?"

Frost scoffed and shook his head. "Keep saying that, bro. Maybe eventually you'll even believe it."

"So—the ride?"

"Yeah. No problem. I have to go put my sound system away, and then I'll meet you out in front of the house in a few."

"Thanks, Frost. I'll owe you one."

"No worries. Just…treat my sister right, okay?"

"Of course."

"Good. I'd hate to have to mess up that pretty smile of yours."

Jake knew Frost was just joking around, and the two of them bumped fists.

Frost went back to loading his equipment, and Jake found his mother and explained his plan to her, giving Lottie a kiss on the cheek and telling her good-night.

Finally, he returned to Avery, who was waiting on the bench they'd used all evening.

"Ready to go?" he said, offering his hand to her as she stood up.

She flipped on her flashlight and teasingly aimed it at his face, causing him to have to shade his eyes.

"See? I told you I had plenty of light to help me find my way home."

"Just humor a Texan gentleman, will you?" He flashed her his best smile.

"Sure. You want me to play damsel in distress?" She threaded her fingers through his and gave his hand a squeeze.

Laughter escaped from his throat. "Somehow, I just can't picture that. You're a lot of things, Avery, but a damsel in distress isn't one of them."

"No, I suppose not. I guess you're stuck with me the way I am, then."

"I like the way you are."

She glanced up at him, and he was glad for the shadows that hid his face, which was burning with heat. Way to go and blab what was really on his mind.

"So—about Sissy," he said attempting to divert her from the topic. "You were telling me you were working with her on becoming an epilepsy service dog. Do you mean specifically for Lottie?"

"Yes, actually." She gracefully followed his change of conversation. "I really think she'll help Lottie manage her condition. Sissy is already trained to stay with her person no matter where she is—class, playground, church. If you agree with me, we can get you and Lottie scheduled to come by for training for an hour every day for two weeks."

"That's what your bed-and-breakfast is for, isn't it?" Jake asked as the light bulb went off in his mind. No wonder she was so adamant about needing such a facility.

"Exactly. It usually takes two weeks of training with the dog's new owners for them to get used to each other and learn all the commands they'll need to know. Having somewhere nearby to stay where they don't have to worry about a room and meals will be very helpful."

"I see," he said.

She stopped and turned toward him. "Do you?"

"Believe it or not, Avery, I'm not a monster. When I started working for Marston, I believed I was doing a good thing, building resorts for families to take vacations at, not to mention making a good living for me and my family. I'm investing my savings so Lottie can go to college if she wants to."

"Of course, and that's a good thing. The problem is your resorts themselves. Guests have to be as rich as Midas. They aren't your everyday families, Jake." She sounded appalled by the thought. "And it works out just fine for you if you don't mind plowing through small towns and changing every nuance of what makes them special."

She didn't have to spell it out for him. He already knew what he and his company were doing to Whispering Pines and numerous other small towns. It had taken a woman like Avery to open his eyes.

But it was too late to redeem himself now.

He was here now, and the changes were already in motion.

"My wife, Amber, used to say the same thing," he said, watching his step as Avery swept the path with the beam of her flashlight. "She's been gone for a while now, but she was stubborn when she wanted to be. She didn't like that I worked for Marston and was always encouraging me to quit. Who knows? I may just have, except I was just as stubborn, and then…"

He choked up and couldn't finish the sentence.

They were approaching the Winslow house, and the lights from inside lit up well beyond the front porch. Avery stopped abruptly and pulled him back, so they were still in the shadow.

"Do you mind me asking what happened to Amber? Or is that too painful for you to talk about?"

In truth it was like a dagger in the heart for him to talk about Amber, but Avery deserved to hear the truth. "That was actually what we were fighting about the day I left town for one of my extended stays in a small town in Utah. Nowadays I bring Lottie and my mom with me wherever I travel, but back then a very pregnant Amber stayed at home when I went out for Marston."

"That's a lot of time apart."

"Which was exactly what Amber kept saying. She gave me an ultimatum, really. She told me I could keep ignoring my family during my climb to the top of my career or I could rethink my priorities. She kept reminding me that we were going to have a daughter, as if I didn't already know that. I was so angry when I left that day. I didn't think she appreciated all I was doing for her."

He paused again. "As it turned out, I was the one who didn't appreciate her."

"Was she ill?"

He shook his head. "No. She was going down the front-porch stairs at our house with her arms laden with new annuals to plant in the flower beds. My best guess is she twisted her ankle and fell onto the cement and hit her head."

Avery gasped.

"I don't know how long she'd been lying there, but I was the one to find her. She was unconscious. I called 9-1-1, and they brought her to the hospital, but she never regained consciousness.

"Since it was about time for Lottie to be born, anyway, she was successfully delivered by C-section. At the time, everything about her seemed normal. Lottie checked out well. But then when she was about six months old, she started having seizures. I'll never know if it was because of Amber's fall or because of her being unconscious.

"If only I had gotten there a few hours earlier, everything might have been different. But I missed my flight and had to take a later one. I wasn't worried about it. I didn't even call Amber and let her know I'd be late. If I had and she hadn't answered, I might have suspected something was wrong. It's my fault. It's all my fault."

He dropped her hand and scrubbed both hands down his face, dashing away the tears that had rolled down his cheeks as his heart squeezed tight in his chest.

"It was an accident," Avery whispered, her voice rough with emotion. She had tears in her eyes, as well.

"You know how the Bible says not to let the

sun go down on your anger? There's a reason that's so important. You may never have another opportunity to tell the ones you care for that you love them. I'll carry that guilt around as long as I live. And every time Lottie has a seizure—it's almost more than I can bear."

"I know this is hard for you to hear right now, but God wouldn't give us more than we can handle," she gently reminded him. "I don't know why He took Amber away, but I do know I've watched you with Lottie, and you're a wonderful father. You might not have had that kind of relationship with her if the Lord hadn't forced your hand."

"I never thought of it that way. My mom and Lottie—they're not a burden to me." He was starting to realize the true burden was his career, not his family. Before Amber had passed away, he'd been an absentee husband and would no doubt have gone on to be an absentee father. He would have missed all the precious moments in his daughter's life.

Now he was dragging Lottie and his mother around everywhere without a bit of stability. Without a real home.

He didn't know how all this was going to

end in Whispering Pines or with Avery, but change was in the wind and he couldn't ignore God's quiet pull on his heart.

They walked into the light shining from the porch, and Avery turned to him. "Well, this is me." She pressed a palm to his well-trimmed beard. "Go easy on yourself."

"Avery, I—" He covered her hand with his own and stepped closer to her, close enough that their breaths mingled. "I don't—I don't know what I'm doing."

He was going to step back again, but she tipped her chin up and met his gaze. "Don't you?" she whispered.

He leaned down until their lips were barely touching, a kiss so soft and gentle it made the whole world still around them.

He half expected her to stop him, to push him away.

"Please," she whispered. Her voice was frayed with emotion.

*Please what?*

But then she lifted her other hand and framed his face, drawing him closer. For a moment, they simply stood forehead to forehead as their gazes met and held.

Their lips met again. His last thought was

of how much his eyes had been opened by this amazing woman.

And then there were no more thoughts.

He melted into her embrace.

## Chapter Ten

Jake's mouth was warm against hers as he kissed her.

Somewhere in the back of her mind, she thought she ought to be pulling away, stopping this before it went any further.

But part of her was reveling in this meeting of hearts. Despite their disagreements, she'd seen so much good in Jake, and she could no longer deny her attraction to him.

He broke off the kiss and pulled her closer, tucking her under his chin. She could hear his heartbeat racing as he tightened his hold on her.

For this one moment, she felt as if she'd been made for him. She fit perfectly in his arms, and their hearts beat in tandem.

"Avery," he whispered. There was a different tone to his voice than earlier. He sounded concerned.

Anxious, even.

He gently took her by the shoulders and leaned back, putting a measure of distance between them. It was only inches, but as far as Avery was concerned, it may as well have been miles.

"Avery. We can't— This isn't—"

Thoughts suddenly raced through her mind. What were they doing here?

Making life more difficult for the both of them, that's what they were doing. No doubt about that.

No matter how good this felt, how right it felt to be in each other's arms, it was leading exactly nowhere.

She took a deep breath and jerked her head once in agreement.

"I know," she said, her voice raw with emotion.

He dropped his hands and stepped back, then lifted his hat and combed his fingers back through his hair.

"I'm sorry. I really am. I shouldn't have—" He shrugged and let his sentence drop without finishing it.

"There's nothing for you to be sorry for," she assured him. "We just got caught up in the moment, that's all. Ice-skating. Fairy lights. Eighties power ballads. Couples' skating. It happens."

Except it *didn't* happen.

Not for Avery.

Not for a really long time.

But she didn't want to put any more pressure on Jake than he was already feeling. She could see in his eyes he was blaming himself.

Anyway, he was right. They shouldn't have gotten caught up in a romantic moment. Falling for him would be the absolute worst thing she could do. Because it wasn't just Jake her heart had to contend with.

It was Lottie, too. And when Jake wrapped things up for Marston and left to move onto the next small town, she would be broken-hearted times two.

It might even already be too late for her. It certainly felt like it right now.

"Frost?" Jake called, and Avery turned to find her brother approaching, his hands jammed in the pockets of his fleece-lined jean jacket and his expression serious.

Her face heated as Frost raised an eyebrow

at her. How long had he been there? What had he heard? Seen? Sometimes it was hard to have so many siblings. It felt like she was practically tripping over them at the most frustrating of times. It was none of Frost's business what she did or didn't do, or with whom.

"You ready to go?" Frost asked Jake.

"Go?" Avery echoed.

"Yeah. Leave. He wanted to walk you home, so now I'm going to take him back to his place."

"Hmmph," Avery said, stepping farther away from Jake. "And you just thought you'd stand there and watch us without making your presence known? Nothing to see here."

"Really? That's not what it looked like to me," Frost said.

Avery wanted to wallop him.

"Frost," said Jake, a warning in his tone. "Can we please just drop it?"

Frost shrugged. "If you say so. Come on. Let's get going."

Jake sent Avery an apologetic look and turned to follow Frost to his truck.

Avery sighed and headed toward the house. It was bad enough that she'd never been so confused in her life, but then Frost had to go and see her kissing Jake. She knew she hadn't heard the last from him. He would tease her incessantly. And of course the news would spread throughout the Winslow house like wildfire.

This was going to be a very long week.

She finally let herself inside the house and was immediately approached by Ruby and Felicity, both of whom had mischievous sparkles in their eyes.

"What?" she asked suspiciously.

"I think that's the answer you should be giving us," Ruby said with a chuckle. "What is going on between you and Jake Cutter?"

"Please don't tell me you two were watching us out the window."

"What? No. Why would we do that? Or *should* we have been peeking? What did we miss? We were actually talking about the couples' skate at the lake. You two looked pretty cozy there for a while, and it was so cute when Lottie skated out to join you," Felicity said.

"What happened that we should have seen out the window? What'd we miss?" Ruby's excitement was rising with every word she spoke as she repeated the question Felicity had just asked.

Lovely. Avery just had to go and open her big mouth.

They'd know soon enough, once Frost got home and talked about what he'd seen. But still.

"Nothing. Absolutely nothing to see out there."

"He kissed you, didn't he?" Felicity guessed. "Oooohhh. I had no idea your relationship had progressed to that point, but I can't say I'm surprised. He's been interested in you since the moment he came to town."

"That is so not true." Avery shook her head, her shoulders tensing tighter with every word. "Can we just not talk about it?"

Immediately, her sisters became serious. "Are you okay? You wanted to kiss him, didn't you? We both thought—"

"Yes," Avery answered. "And no."

Felicity groaned softly. "Relationships can be so complicated, can't they?"

"Tell me about it. Why can't anything be easy for a change? Just once I'd like things to be easy."

"But you like him," Ruby said.

"I do," she admitted. "And Lottie, too. Which is exactly the point. That's why it's so complicated. Do you see the problem here?"

Felicity shook her head and shrugged. "Not really. It's only a problem if you make it a problem."

"I don't have to make it a problem, Felicity. It's already there, right in front of me on several counts. For one thing, I've been in a relationship with a single father and a kid once, and I don't need to remind you how well that turned out for me."

"Jake isn't T.J.," Ruby said. "He's a much better man."

"Well, I'll agree with you on that. But there's still the fact of him working for Marston Enterprises. He's going to win over the town council, and his stupid company is going to raze my perfect bed-and-breakfast cabin. If I spend any time with him and his family, I'm going to grow close to them—all of them. And then he'll take Lottie and leave town in that fancy red Mustang of his, stirring up dust on his wheels on his way out."

"I think you may be overstating things just a bit," Ruby said. "I mean, if he cares for you enough to kiss you, maybe he'll want to stick around."

"How am I overstating?" Avery challenged. "I don't know his timeline, but it can't be that long before he leaves. That's his job, going from place to place to lay the groundwork in building new resorts. Once he's done, then he has no reason to stay. We discussed spending a couple of weeks training Sissy for Lottie's epilepsy, and the town council isn't for another three weeks yet, but then? He's out of here."

"That's three more weeks to see where this relationship might go," suggested Felicity. "And I disagree with you. I think he *does* have a good reason to stay."

"Let me be absolutely clear on one thing," Avery said firmly. "This relationship between Jake and me is going nowhere, and we both know it. I don't know what happened out there tonight, but this is where it stops. We both agreed on that."

"Right," said Ruby, giving her a grin and a nod that suggested she didn't believe a word Avery said.

She didn't have to believe it. Avery would make sure it didn't happen. She wasn't exactly sure how, especially since they had to work closely together to make Sissy and Lottie a team. Every second was going to be more painful than she even wanted to think about. But she knew enough now to put an extra guard around her heart. Jake was obviously doing the same. It was what they had to do.

She went up to her bedroom, changed into her pajamas, slipped into bed and pulled the covers up to her ears, wishing for a moment she could just make the whole world disappear.

But that would mean she'd never met Jake and his family at all, and she just couldn't wish that away, no matter how painful it turned out for her.

Maybe the best thing for her to do would be to drop the fight against Marston altogether. That would be one less thing she'd have to worry about.

It wasn't the first time she'd considered the idea. Yes, it was her dream cabin. It would be hard to let go of it and look for something else. But it wasn't as if she stood even the slightest chance of winning, so eventually she'd be looking for a different cabin, anyway.

And yet she'd heard so many opinions from her friends and neighbors about the issue. She had yet to find one single person who was genuinely enthused about the idea of having a big resort move into the Whispering Pines area. She'd done her research and had her list of endangered plants and animals that had the potential to be affected by Marston's plans.

It wasn't much, but it was something. And she had to do it for the others, if not for herself.

It wasn't just about her, now. She couldn't quit this fight, even if she wanted to.

And for Lottie's sake, she couldn't simply avoid Jake, even if she wanted to.

With tears of frustration welling in her eyes, she rolled over, curling her pillow around her head, and cried herself to sleep.

Jake leaned his hip on the small kitchen table he was currently using as his desk and waited for his portable printer to finish copying flyers for the day's work. He had talked to most of the men and women who led the town council, but he knew that wouldn't be enough. Far from it. From everything Avery had told him, it would be the area's business owners he'd really have to win over if he was going to make this thing work.

It shouldn't be that hard. He'd done it before. He'd put together a one-page presentation of how a Marston resort would help the small businesses in the area expand and prosper and how it would be a big boost for the economy to be stamped with the Marston name. Now he intended to speak to everyone face-to-face and hopefully to put a friendly face with a name.

He never used to doubt his innate charm. He'd made a very good living off it. But charm wasn't enough where Avery Winslow was concerned, and that threw him off his game. It made him question everything he thought he knew about himself.

He hadn't imagined he'd ever be attracted to another woman after Amber, yet he couldn't find it in his heart to regret kissing Avery. For that one moment, he'd been able to let everything go—his guilt, his pain. She'd offered him something he realized he desperately needed—she genuinely cared for him. For his family.

And now he had to walk away. He'd had to be the strong one that night, the one to pull away, or he might never have pulled away from her. That woman deserved the very best in life, a man who could give her everything.

That man wasn't him. He'd lost too much to be able to give her only what was left of his heart. She needed a whole man, not a broken one.

So, he would tuck away the beautiful memory of their kiss and move on with his life. He'd talk to the business owners in town. He would spend the necessary hours with Lottie in training with Sissy. And then he'd leave Whispering Pines and never return.

The printer finished copying his flyers, and he gathered them up and checked his appearance in the mirror. He'd switched back to wearing his suit, and he straightened his tie and adjusted his cowboy hat, knowing how important it was to appear professional.

His first stop was Johnson's Sporting Goods. He'd met Fred Johnson the other day when he'd bought his skates, so he thought that would be a good place to start. He intended to go over the talking points with Fred and then ask if he could put the flyer in the front window of the store.

The bell over the door rang when Jake

entered, and the scent of leather unique to sporting-goods stores hit him. Though he often visited the gym to keep in shape, he'd never been very athletic or played any sports other than baseball, so he didn't feel especially at home in the store. He must have appeared quite lost when he was shopping for his skates, since he'd known nothing about what to look for.

But today, he reminded himself, he was entirely in his element—sales. It was what he did and did well.

He didn't immediately see Fred, and no one came to greet him, so he decided to explore the store and see if he could find Fred or another employee who might know where the owner was.

He finally found Fred behind a counter at the back. Bows and arrows with targets lined the back walls, which caught his interest at first. But suddenly he realized he wasn't alone, which was probably why he hadn't greeted Jake near the front.

Jake immediately recognized the woman dressed in jeans and a mint-green sweater, her blond hair pulled back in a ponytail and looped through an orange-and-blue baseball cap—the Denver Broncos, of course.

*Avery.*

What was she doing here?

As Jake moved closer, he could see there was a flyer laid out on the counter between Avery and Fred, and she was pointing at something on it and speaking in a low voice.

Fred looked up and acknowledged Jake's presence, holding up a finger to let him know he'd be with him in a moment, but Avery didn't so much as glance over her shoulder. She was too busy presenting whatever it was on her flyer that had her so extremely animated.

He moved behind her and glanced over her shoulder so he could see the paper. It was all about the town meeting, which for some reason made Jake hide his own flyers behind him and out of sight.

He didn't know why he did that. It was silly. But it was an impulse he couldn't control.

Avery finished telling Fred about how he should attend the meeting and why—something about saving their town from the big, bad Marston Enterprises, as well as their responsibility to this and that plant and flower and a surprising assortment of wildlife.

And here he stood, listening in on their private conversation.

The big, bad wolf himself.

Marston Enterprises in polished black cowboy boots.

"May I put this flyer in your front window, Fred?" Avery asked.

Her voice alone sent a frisson of awareness down Jake's spine. And he was going to work with her for two weeks so Lottie could get a service dog? How was that going to work out for him when he was so completely mindful of her whenever she was near?

"Sure thing," Fred said. "Please feel free. Do you need tape?"

"I've got some tape you can use," said Jake, stepping forward and offering his roll of tape from his inside jacket pocket.

Avery must have jumped a foot in the air, which gave Jake some sense of satisfaction that he could affect her the same way she affected him.

"Do you always sneak up on people that way?" she demanded, putting her free hand over her heart.

Okay, so maybe it was more that he'd startled her than that she was reacting to his presence in the store. But he'd take his points where he could get them. "I've been standing here for quite some time waiting for my turn," he explained with a grin.

"You…have?" she asked, her face coloring a pretty pink that made Jake's stomach flutter. "How—how much did you hear?"

"Enough." Enough to know she had her own agenda. But then again, he'd known that fact since the first day they'd met. It wasn't as if she ever tried to hide it.

Only now, it was personal.

"Well, I'll be on my way," she squeaked, her voice suddenly high-pitched. "You should have said something about waiting for me to finish here. I don't want to get in the way of one of Fred's paying customers." She looked him straight in the eye. "That'll happen soon enough, now, won't it?"

*Ouch.*

He wanted to snap back at her, but where would that get him? Instead, he clamped his jaw closed to keep from saying something he knew he would later regret. Seeing as she had her own roll of tape, he withdrew his hand with the double-sided tape and shoved it back into his inner jacket pocket. He then watched as she straightened her shoulders and marched—that was the right word, *marched*—to the front and posted her flyer at eye level in the window right next to the front door.

She hadn't brought double-sided tape, so she taped around the outside of the flyer instead. Then she stood back and admired her handiwork.

She didn't even glance back when she left.

He sighed deeply. So, this was how it was going to be between them.

Had he made an enemy the night they'd kissed? Was that the absolute very worst thing he could have done? Or was she just feeling the same hurt he was and was processing and displaying it a different way?

Jake turned back to Fred to explain what he was doing in the shop, although coming in right after Avery, he doubted he was going to get very much traction before Fred politely shut him down and showed him the door.

Surprisingly, Fred allowed him to make his pitch and even agreed to allowing him to put his flyer in the window, but he could tell it was under duress, because Fred was just too nice to say no outright. But Fred's expression and the way he continuously clenched his jaw as if he was chewing gum told Jake all he needed to know about how well his presentation was being taken.

Jake experienced more than one awkward moment when Fred asked the hard questions about why Marston thought they had the right to come into Whispering Pines and build the resort and yet again when he hung his flyer next to Avery's. It felt incredibly awkward, but then, he expected that was exactly what Avery was aiming for.

When he exited Johnson's Sporting Goods, he took a deep breath of the crisp mountain air and glanced up and down the street, wondering where to go next.

The real question was where Avery had gone, because the last thing he wanted to do was follow in her footsteps all day. She already had the advantage of having grown up in this town and knowing nearly everyone here. She was a face they recognized. So now, with every business she got to before him, he would be coming in at a major disadvantage.

He had to hustle or Avery was going to

beat him at every punch. His adrenaline was surging through his veins, but oddly enough, he didn't feel animosity toward Avery. It was frustrating, certainly, but she was doing what she thought best.

That's what they both had to do.

She wouldn't win her fight, but he had to admire the lengths she was going to—to try her best.

# Chapter Eleven

Avery swept up the floor of the dog-training facility and then mopped it with a strong disinfectant, something she and her sisters did morning and evening every day for the sake of both the dogs and the clients who came to meet them.

After that, she laid down a few interlocking rubber mats for training purposes. Avery had been working with Sissy since the day she'd met Jake and Lottie at the pizza parlor and had witnessed exactly what Sissy was able to do for the little girl. Though Sissy appeared to already have the ability to instinctively track seizures, she worked with the dog to consistently alert and respond.

First, she'd lain down on the mat and acted as if she were having an epileptic seizure. It wasn't quite the same because nothing internal was happening that Sissy would be able to sense and pick up on—theoretically that a seizure had some form of scent attached to it—but she managed to get Sissy's interest just by quivering on the floor. Then she encouraged the dog to perform what already came naturally to her—putting pressure on her chest to keep her safe and licking her face to keep her as focused as possible and to let her know that Sissy was there watching over her.

At first, the dog was rewarded with a clicker for immediate reinforcement, followed by a treat because she was very food-motivated, but now Sissy didn't need a physical reward to do what she did best—the work itself was enough of a reward for her.

Wanting to practice one more time before the Cutters arrived for the start of their official training, she set Sissy in place and lay down on the mat. Then she took a deep breath and started her best imitation of a seizure. Sissy immediately alerted and then took her place, offering gentle pressure on Avery's chest and licking her chin.

"Avery?" Jake's concerned Texas drawl cut

through Sissy's kisses. "Avery, honey, are you okay?"

He raced to her side and knelt beside her, brushing her hair off her forehead, an alarmed frown lingering on his lips.

Avery's gaze widened when their eyes met. Jake looked so anxious he appeared as if he was about to jump right out of his skin.

She rolled to her hands and knees and chuckled. "No worries, Jake. I was just training with Sissy on what to do for Lottie's seizures."

Jake blew out a breath as he sat back on his haunches, bracing himself with his palms on his thighs. "Don't scare me like that, woman."

"Sorry." She realized in hindsight what it must have looked like to him when he entered. He had to deal with his daughter's very real grand mal seizures on a regular basis. Of course walking in and seeing Avery on the ground looking as if she was seizing would have thrown him off-balance.

"That's how you do it?" Elaine asked in amazement, joining their little group. "Teach Sissy to respond to seizures by mimicking them yourself?"

"Yes," Avery explained. "I start with treats

because Sissy likes to get a treat when she does something right. By working with me, she learns more or less what a seizure looks like and what the correct alert and response should be. Now, when we start working with her and Lottie together, Sissy will learn even more. And she'll be ready to go when the real thing occurs.

"As we saw at Sally's Pizza, Sissy instinctively responded to Lottie's seizure. She appeared to know it was going to happen even before Lottie did. There's a theory that it has something to do with a scent, since dogs' noses pick up so much more than ours. In any case, when Lottie's seizures happen, Sissy will continue to learn to always be aware of the possibility, she'll hone her senses specifically for Lottie, and she'll always be there to keep her eye on her. So—are you ready to start your training?"

At first Avery had the adults sit in folding chairs in a circle with Lottie and Sissy playing together in the middle while she discussed what it meant to own and care for a service dog in general and Sissy in particular. Being a golden retriever, she was a medium-size dog and would need to have regular exercise.

"Lottie and I take a long walk every day," Elaine assured her. "It's part of our regular routine. It will be lovely to take Sissy along with us. Or Jake can take her with him when he runs. I'm sure having Sissy around is something we'll all enjoy."

Lottie squealed when Sissy sniffed her and tickled her under the chin with her cold nose.

"I honestly never thought we'd have a pet," Jake admitted. "Seeing as we travel around so much. Even though Lottie kept begging for a dog, it never seemed like the right time. But I assure you we'll make this work no matter what it takes. Sissy will be part of the family, not just a service dog."

"That's wonderful to hear," Avery admitted. "Not every service dog ends up in a family such as yours. Sissy was born to do a job, but she's still a dog who deserves to live with a loving family. That's super important to us when we place a dog here at our training program. Sissy will be a constant companion for Lottie. She'll enjoy hanging out on the couch with Lottie while she watches cartoons on TV and will cuddle up with her on the bed when she sleeps at night, giving her extra comfort and safety. Obviously, it's really important that Sissy accompanies Lottie everywhere—to school, to church, out shopping. Everywhere."

"I am so impressed by all of this," Elaine exclaimed, clapping her hands under her chin. "You have no idea how much good you do in the world."

"I do," said Jake, his voice gruff with emotion.

Avery glanced at him, stunned by his words.

"I mean, you haven't said a word to pat yourself on the back for all you've done," he said, running his hand across his jaw, "but I know you've gone to a ton of effort to get Sissy ready for Lottie on such short notice. I—*we*—appreciate that more than we can express."

"Of course. No question. I'm happy to do it."

Their gazes met again, and she wondered if he could tell where her mind had gone—to the perfect little cabin that would make such a good bed-and-breakfast for clients just like them, people who needed the services A New Leash on Love provided.

Avery watched Lottie and her new dog for a moment and smiled softly. Maybe Jake would see it now. This was what they were all about.

This kind of connection.

This kind of love.

It might be the only kind of love Avery would be able to experience—now, and maybe for a long time to come. She suspected her heart wasn't going to automatically right itself once Jake went away.

But knowing at the end of the process she was sending Lottie away with Sissy, and that Sissy would take care of the little girl—it was all worth it.

Because Avery knew right now it wasn't about her.

She had no idea if what he'd seen today would have any impact upon Jake. She wasn't even sure Jake could back down from Marston Enterprises' position even if he wanted to, what with the large corporation behind him, pushing him on to succeed as he always did.

But it couldn't hurt to pray that today had made a difference in his thinking and his heart.

\* \* \*

Jake couldn't even come up with words to express his appreciation for what Avery had done for Lottie with Sissy's assistance. It was truly amazing.

Avery showed the Cutters how to practice with Sissy to prepare her for her new job, and Lottie and Elaine made several practice runs with the dog, who behaved beautifully and consistently. Jake was still bewildered by the fact that a dog could sense an epileptic seizure at all, much less respond to it in a positive way that was truly helpful. Sissy would quite literally change Lottie's whole life, giving her a new sense of freedom as she grew up and eventually went to school.

Jake gently took Avery's elbow and motioned her aside so he could speak to her in private.

"What do I owe you for Sissy?" he whispered for her ears only. "I can pay you right now, tonight, so you don't have to go through all the trouble of sending an invoice. Please include both the training and the dog herself. And just for the record—I'm a big tipper."

He flashed her one of his signature grins, but naturally she didn't respond to it. If anything, her brow lowered, and her lips curved into a frown.

Typical Avery. Was there nothing that made her happy other than the cabin that would soon be completely unavailable for purchase?

"What?" he asked guardedly, wondering what the problem was now.

"We don't sell our service dogs," she told him in a no-nonsense tone with a narrow-eyed glare for punctuation.

"What?" he asked, confused. "I don't— How does A New Leash on Love run if not by selling the dogs you train?"

"It's a ministry," she informed him tightly. "There are so many people who need what we provide that we determined early on when we first started rescuing and training dogs that it would never be about money."

"I see," he said, although he didn't really get it at all. "So it's—what? A nonprofit organization?"

"Yes."

"But even nonprofits that adopt out dogs and cats charge for what they do."

She nodded. "Most of them do. But they

aren't us." She lifted her chin and narrowed her gaze. "This is how we serve God."

He wasn't about to argue with God.

"Well, then, may I donate to your non-profit?" he asked in the lightest possible tone. He didn't want to offend her further or send her into a snit, but he did want to contribute to her program. It was wonderful that they donated service dogs to whoever needed them, but he could afford to pay, and he wanted to. "I see what a difference you make, and I'd really like to help."

He was afraid to move even so much as a muscle as her gaze ran over him, testing his mettle.

"Please, Avery," he said. "I can afford it. And what you do here—I get that it's a ministry, and your dogs are beyond amazing. I'd like to help you all keep it going."

"So, you're not the widow offering her last mite, then."

One thing he had to say for Avery—she was snark personified. But for some reason that was one of the things he liked about her. She called it as she saw it with a little sarcasm to spice it up.

He chuckled. "Hardly. Nor will it be left

and right hands doing things in secret the other one doesn't know about. I've always been too straightforward in my philanthropy. Trust me, it won't dent my pocketbook at all. And since you're a nonprofit, I can write it off on my taxes. Win-win as far as I'm concerned."

"Yes, okay, you can make a donation. I'll tell you what. I'll send you an email with the relevant details for you to make a credit card donation online."

"That's perfect," he said. Better than perfect, actually, because he'd be able to make ongoing donations that way, which he thoroughly intended to do.

"Avery! Jake!" his mother called, waving them over. "Hurry! Come see!"

Jake's heart leapt into his throat, afraid Lottie was having another seizure, and as he and Avery approached, that was exactly what it looked like was happening. Jake was about to rush into action to take care of his little girl, but Avery stopped him with a hand on his arm.

"Look," she whispered. "Watch what's happening."

Jake observed the scene unfolding in

front of him with a sense of wonder. As he watched, he realized there was something different about what was happening right before his eyes.

Lottie wasn't having a seizure, or at least, not a real one. She was mimicking what she'd seen Avery do earlier, and Sissy was responding perfectly, whining an alert and then lying down lengthwise at Lottie's side with one paw over her, licking her chin to let her know the dog was with her.

"This will never get old," Jake murmured. "Sissy is going to make so much difference in all of our lives."

"Yes, she will," Avery agreed. "I'll be drawing up the adoption papers to make it official, but in the meantime, Lottie, do you want to take Sissy home with you to be your new best friend?"

"What do you think, sweetie? Should we take Sissy home with us?" Jake asked, his heart racing so fast he knew it must show in his expression.

There were no words.

Lottie was now wiggling and squealing in a whole different way, joyfully throwing her arms around Sissy's neck and hugging her tightly.

"Let me get Sissy's service-dog vest, which you'll want her to wear whenever you go out. It helps put Sissy in the right frame of mind to know she's supposed to be working. Also, let me put together a welcome kit with some kibble and other things you'll need as new dog owners. Once you get back to Dallas, you'll want to see a vet and establish a relationship with them."

Jake followed Avery around as she moved from place to place putting the care package together.

A dog owner. He'd never had a pet before, not even when he was a child. Becoming a young widow after his father had died in his early thirties and having to work two jobs to support herself and Jake, his mother had always believed it wouldn't be fair to add a cat or a dog to the family. But now, with Sissy, the dog wasn't just going to be a part of the family. She was going to be Lottie's friend and protector.

"You'll need to bring Sissy with you back here to the training center every night for the next two weeks so we can work on alert and response specifically geared toward Lottie," Avery informed him, tossing a genuine smile over her shoulder. "It's convenient for you that you're temporarily living nearby, don't you think?"

He hadn't expected that barb aimed at him to hit him right in the heart, but perhaps he should have. Despite how generous she was with Sissy and Lottie, there was this one big thing between them.

After what he'd seen tonight, there was no question that he agreed with Avery. A nearby bed-and-breakfast would be beyond helpful in more ways than even Avery probably dreamed about. He was seeing the other side now, receiving A New Leash on Love's services. Not everyone would have the resources he had available to him, and Avery wanted the cabin as a way to help them.

Jake would personally have done anything to help.

But Marston wasn't going to listen to anything Jake had to say. And they weren't going to give the least bit of consideration to Avery's personal feelings or whatever scraps of data and research she came up with to fight them when it came to going head-to-head at the town council.

She was going to lose.

Could he really let that happen?

# Chapter Twelve

Avery adjusted the maroon silk scarf knotted around her neck for the tenth time in as many minutes. Her sisters had insisted her wearing a business suit—a navy blue skirt and jacket with a pristine white blouse—would be the best choice for going up against Marston. Whispering Pines might be a small mountain town, but Avery would look professional. And maybe the outfit would lend her the courage she was so desperately seeking and couldn't seem to find.

She was going to have to fake it.

Ruby and Felicity had secretly bought the outfit as a gift to her and had presented it to her the previous evening. At the time, she'd graciously accepted it, appreciating the thought behind it, but now she thought it felt like overkill. She looked more like a flight attendant than someone prepared to take on the big-league lawyers sitting to her right, fiddling with their expensive briefcases and color-coded file folders.

Avery had exactly one plain manila file folder in her possession, and she'd hand-carried that in. Even if it had occurred to her to use one, she didn't even own a briefcase, and the backpack she generally used to tote items definitely wouldn't have matched her outfit.

Her brothers and sisters were in the row directly behind her, but she felt as if she were physically shrinking just standing there all by herself at the table. Maybe she should have brought in the local lawyer, even if his specialty was family practice and he wouldn't have had the first clue what to do in this situation.

Someone had set up a single row of rectangular tables and chairs across the front of the room and the town council was gathering behind it. On the left side facing the council, Avery stood behind a single, bare table with only her one file folder on it. A half-dozen lawyers were standing around their table, buzzing quietly to each other.

Everyone looked prepared and ready to go. The only person missing was Jake. Avery glanced back at the crowded room but didn't see him anywhere. She'd assumed he'd be front and center in all this. It was all his doing, after all.

The town mayor, Paul Dillinger, came out from around the front tables and approached Avery, leaning his hip against the front of her table and flashing her an encouraging smile.

"What do you think, Avery? Are you ready to sling your stone and topple Goliath over there?"

Avery chuckled. The mayor had flat out said he was rooting for her, as had the majority of the council in whose hands was the final decision regarding whether or not Marston could build the resort in their town.

She'd heard from so many townsfolk who didn't want to see the changes Marston Enterprises would bring in. It encouraged her to know how they felt, but at the end of the day it didn't change anything. If she couldn't make an airtight case against Marston building over her future bed-and-breakfast, it was going to happen. Because no matter how the members of the council personally felt, they had to follow the town ordinances and act in what the law considered the best interests of the town.

She had a few stones in her pouch to be used in her proverbial sling, but they were small at best. She wasn't sure she could even bruise the brute that was Marston, much less knock them out.

But she had to try.

She'd been praying all day, putting all her trust in God that tonight would turn out as He willed, even if it wasn't what she desired. But it was so hard, especially now that the moment had come.

"I'm going to do my best, Paul, but you're right," she told the mayor. "It's David against Goliath. Look at me with my one flimsy file folder compared to—" she pointed at the table overrun with briefcases, folders and chatty lawyers "—that."

"Don't let them intimidate you with their fancy suits," Paul advised. "Just keep your eyes on us. Talk to us and not to them. Remember, you've known me and the council members your whole life. I know it doesn't look great right now, but you know we're going to take your arguments into serious consideration. I promise."

Avery's throat choked with emotion. "Thanks, Paul. I really appreciate it."

He shook her hand and returned to his place in the middle of the long table facing the community.

She squared her shoulders and sat down at her table, reminding herself that she could have dropped the issue before it had ever come into being here at all. If it was just her own battle, she would have given up long ago and dealt with her personal disappointment herself. One cabin, even one as perfect as the Meyers' place was to her, wasn't worth the kind of fight that was about to go down tonight.

But this was about the people behind her, those in her town who would stand to lose virtually everything if Marston won. Friends who had approached her and begged for her to make a stand for them because they would lose their businesses and their livelihoods to the kinds of shops and stores that would move in along with a high-end resort.

Avery had done her research, spoken to other people in small towns where Marston

Enterprises had swept in and changed everything. This wasn't a vain threat.

She'd been warned.

Apart from the grave possibility of losing their means of support, the folks in Whispering Pines didn't want to become the next Aspen. They liked the small-town vibe, and they didn't want to change it.

Paul pounded a gavel to quiet the chattering crowd. "Pipe down, people, and let's get started here."

*Where was Jake?*

It made no sense that he would have gone to all the trouble to have been the face of Marston Enterprises up to this point and then not even show up at the council meeting. Or maybe his job was over now?

Maybe he'd rather just not be here at all, knowing what was about to go down.

Why did that leave her with such an empty feeling in her chest?

As the crowd quieted, Avery glanced back one last time.

Jake confidently strode up the aisle, Elaine, Lottie and Sissy just behind him. He was dressed in the same suit she'd first seen him in, right down to the obsidian cuff links, but unlike the other Marston employees, he didn't carry a briefcase. One thin file folder similar to Avery's was tucked under one arm.

It probably contained the information that would guarantee a win, just in case the rest of the lawyers couldn't offer a knockdown presentation that would take her out. Jake nodded at her as he passed, but his usual toothy grin was conspicuously missing, his eyebrows were knotted and she could see his clenched jaw.

Elaine smiled and waved as she took a seat just behind the Marston table. Before she could stop the little girl, Lottie pulled away from her grip and dashed across the aisle to throw herself at Avery, wrapping her little arms tightly around her neck and giving her an enthusiastic squeeze and a kiss on the cheek. Sissy sensed the excitement and likewise leaped, her front paws on Avery's shoulder as she kissed away the tears that had sprung to Avery's eyes the moment Lottie had hugged her.

*No tears.*

*Not now.*

"Miss Avery! Miss Avery! Did you see Daddy?" Lottie asked, her enthusiasm leaking through every syllable. "Isn't he handsome?"

Avery nodded and swallowed hard. How could she not, with his grand entrance—one she now wondered if he'd planned. As it was, she could barely take her eyes off him.

"He is very handsome, sweetheart," she agreed, and, unfortunately for her, she meant it with every beat of her heart.

Elaine apologized profusely as she plucked Lottie away and brought her back to the other side of the aisle. Avery commanded Sissy into a down-stay by Elaine's side.

"I'm so sorry. I didn't expect Lottie to react like that, although I suppose I should have. You are her favorite person right now, since you gave her Sissy."

"It's no problem," Avery insisted, although it very much was. She'd been prepared to see Jake tonight—or at least, she thought she'd equipped her heart well enough to maintain radio silence as she climbed over the present hurdle with Marston.

She could cry her heart out when she was back home in her own bed where no one would see or hear her.

But Lottie throwing herself into Avery's

arms had come as such a surprise, it threw her for a mental and emotional loop she never could have imagined. It went beyond sweet as Avery's heart reached out to Lottie.

Her lungs burned with emotion as she struggled to keep it all in. The very thing she was most afraid of happening had happened.

She loved this little girl.

The mayor pounded his gavel once again and announced the official start of the council meeting. Usually there were one or two minor issues and very few townspeople in attendance. Tonight it was standing room only, as Marston's resort would affect nearly every person in town in one way or another.

Avery returned her thoughts to the fight before her, opening her file folder and glancing through her notes, few as they were. There wasn't much to go on. She had spent days researching what she could in terms of zoning, trying to find reasons Marston couldn't build specifically on the Meyers' property Avery so wanted to claim as her future bed-and-breakfast, and in more general terms, in Whispering Pines at all. She had spoken to people from other towns, gathered witness statements about the many peripheral changes that could and would happen with the coming of Marston's resort and how they wouldn't suit Whispering Pines at all.

Her palms were moist, and her breath was coming in rapid bursts. She worked in the office behind the scenes for a reason, and the thought of getting up and speaking to the entire town was making her feel sick to her stomach.

"We're here today to address the issue of Marston Enterprises building an upscale resort here within Whispering Pines' boundaries," Paul announced. "Because this is such a large and complex issue, I'm going to dispense with the usual formalities and jump right into it."

Paul looked down the line of Marston lawyers until his gaze landed on Jake. "Jake, since you've been around the past couple of months and most of us have met you or at least are familiar with you, why don't you present for Marston?"

Jake tunneled his fingers through his dark hair and glanced at Avery, who was staring straight back at him, her face heating when their gazes met.

*Breathe*, she reminded herself.

After an extended moment, he turned his attention to the mayor and council at the front of the room.

"Well, sir," he said, his Texas drawl especially pronounced, "generally, I'd be happy to take the lead."

Of course he would. Unlike Avery, Jake was a bona fide people person who resonated with crowds. He loved to speak. It didn't matter if it was one person or a thousand. He would easily crush her with his charming smile and slick words, cutting through any arguments she might offer like a sharp ax.

Avery cringed as she realized her Goliath wasn't all the lawyers behind the table trying to look all professional and intimidating.

It was Jake.

And he was completely in his element here.

Jake felt completely out of his element, and he couldn't imagine why.

Actually, he could, and her name was Avery Winslow.

Usually, he thrived on speaking in public. This is what he did for a living—met and won over members of the small towns and then, at the town council meetings, he would close the deal for Marston.

*Bam!*

But when he glanced across the aisle and his gaze met Avery's, the *bam* was a sucker punch right to his stomach, especially when he saw Lottie run to Avery and give her a big hug and kiss. His daughter could not possibly know that to Avery, her daddy was the big, bad wolf personified.

Avery had changed his life in so many ways. And it wasn't just that he didn't want to hurt her—although he would if Marston won the right to build. It didn't take much to imagine her expression when they razed her precious cabin.

Sad?

Yes. She'd be brokenhearted over not being able to remodel the Meyers' cabin into her perfect bed-and-breakfast.

But more than that, she'd be good and angry. And that was something he was fairly certain he'd never be able to overcome. No amount of explaining would change whose side he was on.

"I'd like to defer to Miss Winslow," Jake said, gesturing toward Avery.

"What?" asked one of the senior partners of the law firm that represented Marston. "What are you playing at here, Jake?"

He shrugged. "I'm not."

Actually, he very much was.

But he was going to give Avery a chance to speak first. If she didn't go now, she would see Marston's presentation, and it would likely overwhelm her. Jake didn't want that. It was only fair to give her a fighting chance.

"I—uh— Okay," Avery said as she stood. Jake could tell Avery was nervous and that he'd caught her off guard. But the town needed to hear all she'd done on their behalf, and that meant letting her go first.

He gave her an encouraging smile, which resulted in having her glare back at him, not that he could blame her.

"Okay." He was impressed at how quickly she pulled herself together. "We all know how important the issue we're addressing here tonight is. It affects nearly everyone who lives in Whispering Pines in one way or another. And I'll admit up front that for many, Marston Enterprises building a high-level resort here would benefit their businesses and personal lives substantially. The grocery store.

Johnson's Sporting Goods. Other businesses could adapt to welcome the rich and famous. Like Aspen and other places where Marston has opened resorts, new businesses would likely come rolling in which might, theoretically at least, be good for our economy as a whole. The resort will open up new jobs. And I'm sure everyone has considered how exciting it would be to get to see some of your favorite actors or singers face-to-face. It's tempting to put a lot of emphasis on that."

*Wait, what?*

Jake's gaze flew to Avery, positive he couldn't possibly have heard her right. But she met his gaze with her own determined look and lifted her chin, turning back toward the council and taking a big breath before continuing.

None of this made sense. Why was she here, if not to fight Marston tooth and nail and give it everything she had to make sure the resort never happened?

"However…"

Ah, here it was.

It was all Jake could do not to lean back in his chair, cross his arms and grin from ear to ear. Everyone was about to get a huge dose of Avery's heart, something even the lawyers for Marston wouldn't be expecting.

"Whispering Pines," she continued, "is so much more than numbers on paper or a computer spreadsheet. It is neighbors gathering together on the community green for a Fourth of July picnic and fireworks. It is elementary schoolchildren growing up, going to college and returning to teach the next generation. It is walking into a store and every employee knowing you by name."

*Yes!*

Jake wanted to fist-pump. She was rocking it—making it personal—and it *was* personal, for everyone in this room who didn't work for Marston.

"Celebrities and superstars may choose to walk down the main streets of town and check out what Whispering Pines is all about—but they won't see what we see. They won't feel what we feel. Not only will fancy new shops move in but so will all the people looking to find employment at the resort. We will lose everything that makes our little town unique. The tiny, old-fashioned shops. Neighbors and friends who know and love each other. Worshipping at our small community church every Sunday and fellowshipping afterward. I'm not saying a megachurch is wrong or bad. But I don't think it represents who we are as a town, do you?"

Jake watched the various council members as their expressions changed. This was hitting home, right in their hearts. But they weren't just moved by what Avery had said—they were concerned about what they hadn't yet heard—Marston's side of the issue.

"Is that everything, Miss Winslow?" the mayor asked.

"Not quite," she answered, flipping open her file folder. "I also have some information to present on various endangered plant and animal species that you'll find in and around the area where Marston Enterprises wishes to build. I believe these should be taken into serious consideration."

Jake nearly burst with pride as she presented her line items, different plants and animals that made the area around Whispering Pines their home, including some she'd seen and documented directly on the Meyers' property.

"I'd especially like to point out the number of Rocky Mountain columbines growing on the Meyers' property and elsewhere around the area. Do you think those flying in from other parts of the United States and the world will know—or even care—that the columbine is our state flower and is therefore protected under law? We here in Whispering Pines know it's illegal to pick one of these rare and delicate flowers on public land, which includes the hiking areas Marston Enterprises has built into their plans. But I suspect Marston hasn't given a single thought to the columbine's meaning."

She paused and took another breath. "Gold for Colorado's mining history. Blue for the sky. And the white represents snow."

It was a good argument. A great one, actually.

But it wouldn't be enough.

# Chapter Thirteen

Avery felt as if she'd been talking forever, and yet she wondered if she'd said enough. She suspected not even close. She'd brought out every belief and contention she had, both provable data and the personal thoughts and emotions that she'd encountered as she'd ridden this enormous tidal wave that was Marston Enterprises.

She knew her maelstrom of emotions would hit her eventually, but for the moment she was holding up better than she'd thought she would. She'd managed to make a fairly professional presentation, brief though it was.

It didn't help that at least one of the Marston lawyers was smirking at her, which in her opinion was quite unprofessional. The man couldn't possibly be aware he just motivated her to fight harder, but Jake clearly did. He glanced from the smirking lawyer to Avery, winked slyly and shook his head.

*The guy isn't worth your consideration*, Jake's eyes seemed to say.

Not that it mattered. Avery was finished. She had nothing left to say. She'd presented everything she had, thrown every stone she had in her proverbial pouch. And those representing Marston didn't even look as if what she'd said had made the slightest bit of difference.

She realized with a stab of disappointment that it probably hadn't. But all she could do was her best, and that she'd done. With all her heart and then some.

"I want to thank each member of the council and you, Mayor Dillinger, for taking the time to hear my concerns."

And then she sat down. Her arguments were finished.

She was a bundle of snapping nerves as it was, but those electrical impulses accelerated when Mr. Smirky Lawyer popped up with a remote control in his hand and turned on his PowerPoint display.

Why wasn't Jake making this presentation?

And why hadn't she thought of using a PowerPoint presentation?

Avery had just assumed Jake would be the one to close the deal, since he'd been working so hard to make alliances here in town. Friends, he called them, but Avery couldn't quite let herself believe that, despite how close she'd become to Jake and his family.

Not with what he was about to do to them now.

Instantly, the screen they'd placed up front, carefully angled in the corner so both the townspeople and, far more important, the mayor and the council members could see their slides, starting with their brand logo, a royal blue background with gold calligraphy letters *M* and *E* swirling in and through each other.

"First," said the gray-suited lawyer in a surprisingly high tone of voice, sounding nothing like Jake's warm baritone with his Texas accent, "I would like to thank Miss... uh..."

"Winslow," Jake supplied in a droll tone, crossing his arms over his chest. "Miss Avery Winslow."

"Right. Yes. Miss Winslow. Thank you for

bringing up your concerns to the town council and to us. I believe we can lay those fears to rest in the next twenty minutes and help the Whispering Pines community understand just how good a Marston Enterprises resort will be for your sleepy little town."

Avery raised her eyebrows. Did the lawyer not even realize that he was slamming the beautiful little town in which they all lived—and, consequently, the people who chose to live here? It was one thing not to remember her name—although Avery suspected he had done that on purpose. But to call their town *sleepy*? He couldn't possibly realize what a compliment that was to the people here.

"My name is Victor Layton," the lawyer continued. "You can call me Vic. And I'm proud to represent the premier in resort companies. I'm sure after you see all we can offer you, you'll be happy to welcome us into this community."

Avery bit her lip to keep from saying what was on her mind—that there was nothing they could say or do to change what she thought about Marston. If Jake couldn't do it, this fast-talking Vic wouldn't be able to, either.

Then again, he might be able to persuade others in the community, especially the town council. And that was what it was all about now, wasn't it?

"Before I start my slideshow," Vic continued, "I would like to assure Miss Winslow and the general council that the Rocky Mountain columbines—" he stopped and smirked right at Avery "—will be in good hands with Marston. Now that you've made that particular issue so clear to us," Vic said and met Avery's gaze and narrowed his eyes, "we will be certain to do our research on the issue and deal with it properly."

Vic glanced back at the other lawyers at the table, one of whom was entirely focused on his laptop, no doubt looking for ways to get around the pesky issue of how to deal with the state flower.

"You can assure us that your guests won't pick the flowers?" Avery asked, her eyebrows raised, then realized she was out of order and clamped her jaw closed and crossed her arms.

Vic didn't have to answer her question as he had the floor, but he looked straight at Avery and nodded once. "Nothing a few well-placed signs can't fix."

Avery desperately wanted to argue, but she'd already made her case, and it was quickly going down like a sinking ship.

"Please allow me to start my video presentation here, and then I'll take any questions the mayor and council might have afterward. I'm also happy to open the floor to our many guests tonight," he said, making a sweeping gesture toward the gathered townspeople. "So please, feel free to address any issues you come across this evening."

Avery continued to clench her jaw as Vic started a professionally created PowerPoint presentation, which not only showed graphs and charts full of information about how the town would benefit from the resort but slide after slide of happy faces, people from other towns where Marston Enterprises had built, sound bites from supposed business owners who had profited from the resorts.

Avery wanted to slink under the table. It hadn't even occurred to her to make a visual presentation. Why hadn't she thought of that? Of course Marston was going to come in with guns blazing. And there she was with her one dinky little file folder.

She'd not only let herself down, but she'd

let down the townspeople gathered behind her, those who had begged her to fight for them.

Her words meant nothing in the grand scheme of things. Not when she was up against happy faces and cheerful sound bites.

She carefully watched the expressions on the faces of the council. She didn't believe they'd been taken in by the fancy presentation alone, but all those charts and graphs? All that crunched data Marston was waving around as if it were the answer to everything? All the sound bites of business owners who thought Marston was the best thing that had ever happened to them?

They'd have to take all that into consideration. They'd have to set aside their feelings and emotions and judge what was best for the town.

The only question was, What was that?

Even Avery wasn't sure she knew.

Jake couldn't keep his eyes off Avery's face, his heart aching as her expression grew dimmer and dimmer. He forced himself to release his tight jaw as he tucked his clenched fists under his biceps so no one would see.

He'd known all this was coming, Marston and their stupid sound bites.

He was usually the one who delivered the final blow.

Tonight he'd blatantly refused to be that man.

That was part of the reason Vic was tripping over himself as he spoke. He wasn't used to having to do the dirty work. He wasn't the voice of Marston.

Though Jake wasn't the one who'd created the PowerPoint, he'd seen this presentation dozens of times before—the happy faces, the cheery sound bites of people who were just *so glad* a Marston resort had moved into their towns and changed everything.

But he knew the truth.

He'd *seen* the truth.

And it was in his pocket.

He'd talked to many of these people face-to-face and had heard how their businesses had been damaged when new shops with much more money behind them pushed them into bankruptcy and shuttered their doors. He'd watched rude celebrities acting however they wished, creating all kinds of havoc with the small-town atmosphere.

The entire PowerPoint presentation took a total of twenty minutes. When it was finished, Vic glanced at Jake.

"Do you want to take it from here, buddy?" he asked under his breath.

Jake raised his eyebrows and then grinned. "Actually, yes."

Avery gaped, clearly stunned, as Jake took the lead and moved into the center of the aisle. He smiled at her in encouragement, but not surprisingly, she didn't return the gesture.

Why would she?

She believed he was about to slam-dunk her.

The room was pin-drop quiet as everyone waited for him to speak.

Rather than addressing the council, however, he turned to the townspeople crowding the room and spoke directly to them.

"I'm happy to say I believe I've met most everyone here in the room tonight. It's been my very great privilege to have spent the last few weeks in Whispering Pines with my family. During this time, I have spent time at church, gone ice-skating and in general gotten the pulse of the town. I understand what bringing a Marston resort here would mean."

Avery scoffed under her breath, her brows lowering as she glared at him.

"Because of this, if you would permit me a few more minutes, I'd like to present an additional PowerPoint tonight."

"What?" Vic barked. "What do you think you are you doing, Cutter?"

He met Vic's gaze square on while simultaneously removing a thumb drive from his slacks pocket. "I'm telling these people the truth."

Vic scrambled for the laptop that he'd used to present the PowerPoint on, but Jake reached it first and shoved the thumb drive into the USB. Vic reached for it, but Jake grabbed his wrist and pushed him away.

"Back off, Vic, if you know what's good for you."

Physically, Jake was a good deal larger than Vic. Not that there was any way Jake would ever let it turn into a wrestling match, but should that happen, Jake knew he would win hands down. But it wouldn't come to that. Jake's glare was more than enough to make Vic stand down.

"Ladies and gentlemen, I appreciate your time here tonight," Jake said smoothly. "And I appreciate the extra time you're giving me to speak with you. You've probably all guessed that when I first came to Whispering Pines, my job was to figure out what we'd need in order to make Marston's resort a reality."

He paused and shot one of his award-winning smiles, first toward the crowd and then toward Avery, although she clearly wasn't buying it for a second.

"But then I met everyone. I shared in your church worship and fellowship. I visited your shops and restaurants—Johnson's Sporting Goods and Sally's Pizza, where I was treated not as a customer but as a friend. And I can't begin to describe what that meant to me and my family."

He shook his head at all the pleasant memories. "I was absolutely amazed that you all even let the Winslows train their dogs around town, including in church. That takes a special kind of town."

After a slight bit of definitely suspicious and lightly scattered applause, Jake lifted his hands to quiet the room.

"I realized what I was doing—what Marston was doing—would change everything here. Everything that makes this town special. All the things I really liked about Whispering Pines would go away within months of opening of the resort. So I decided for once in my life I needed to stand up and be honest with myself—and you—about what this really means.

"I went back to some of the towns where Marston has built their resorts and interviewed actual residents to find out the truth about what really happens when Marston moves in. I was surprised by what I heard, and I'd like to share that with you now."

As he turned on his PowerPoint presentation, he glared down at Vic, daring him to speak up or try to stop him. The lawyer looked as if he wanted to but thought better of it.

Jake's presentation wasn't nearly as long as Marston's had been. Mostly it was faces and sound bites. Real people with real problems caused by Marston resorts moving into their small towns. Not a lot of fancy graphs and tables, although he did share some data on the damage Marston had done.

After he turned off the presentation, he turned to the council. "That's the truth. People—and whole towns—have been wrecked by Marston. Not only that, what Avery shared with you tonight is absolutely true. Endangered plants and animals aren't even a blip on Marston's radar. They may pretend to care about the environment if it gets them what they need, but at the end of the day, it's all about the bottom line."

He glanced at Avery, wondering how she was taking all of this. It was all for her, of course. If not for her blowing into his life like a hurricane, he would never have seen Whispering Pines through her eyes. He wouldn't have realized he was making the same mistakes he'd been making for years and realized the way he was hurting people in the process.

He'd been completely blind to what Marston was doing—what he'd been doing. But now he knew the truth, and he was going to stand for that truth, even though it was definitely going to cost him his job.

He had other ideas about how to spend his time, though. Better ways.

His future lay completely in the hands of the woman across from him, who'd stood up when he finished his presentation, her hand across her throat and a stunned expression on her face.

He'd definitely surprised her.

He'd meant to, which was why he hadn't said anything before now. In hindsight, perhaps that hadn't been the best way to handle it. She'd had to sit through Vic's presentation believing he was slicing her to bits.

But the council and the crowd had needed to see Marston's bogus presentation so that when they saw what Jake submitted as the truth, they would recognize that they were being taken and understand exactly why they needed to reject Marston's offer posthaste, however tempting a temporary jolt in their economy might be in the short term.

The fate of Whispering Pines depended on the mayor and the council knowing and acting upon the truth.

And Jake depended on Whispering Pines staying the way it was. Because he'd come to love this small town with all its friendly people, the small, welcoming community church and, most of all, the Winslow family.

Avery in particular.

He planned to have his own family—him, his mother and Lottie—call Whispering Pines their permanent home.

But first, there was something he had left to do.

# Chapter Fourteen

Avery was shocked beyond words. Fortunately, no one had called upon her to speak, so she had time to gather her wits about her.

When Jake had stood up, she was expecting her worst nightmare to come to life. Vic had done a reasonable job of presenting Marston's side of the issue, but that was nothing next to what she knew Jake would be able to do when given the opportunity. He'd taken the time to get to know the people of Whispering Pines. He wasn't just a face who'd suddenly appeared to argue a point. He was someone they'd spoken with, worshipped with, fellowshipped with. His opinion would make a difference.

She'd believed he would bring it home.

That he would close the deal once and for all.

He'd closed the deal, all right.

There was no way Marston would be building in this town. Not after everything Jake had just done to save it. Not one council member would listen to a word Vic or any of the other Marston lawyers had to say, nor would they give any weight to the presentation Vic had given.

All those lawyers in their fancy suits and leather briefcases were sitting in their seats looking at least as dumbfounded as Avery felt. One of their own had turned on them in a major way.

They had nothing left to say, no way to turn this to their advantage. Jake had made sure of that.

Mayor Dillinger spoke up. "Jake, I'd like to thank you for being so candid with us this evening. I think we all know," he said, gesturing to both the council and the townspeople, "what a sacrifice you've personally made to present this information to us tonight, and we want you to understand what it means to us that you chose to stand up and tell the truth."

"You're gonna burn, Cutter," Vic spit out.

"Eh," Jake said with a shrug. "This is Whispering Pines, Colorado, in late winter.

All I've gotta do is stop, drop and roll and I'll be good. The snow will extinguish any worries I might have."

Avery knew she was gaping. Did Jake seriously not realize what was happening here? He was as good as fired from Marston. The moment this meeting was adjourned, calls would be made, and Jake's employment—something with enough benefits to make it possible for him to purchase Mustangs and high-end suits with obsidian cuff links—would be gone in an instant.

She'd never witnessed an act of such bravery in her life. He had stood and told the truth, even if it meant his whole life would now crash down around him. The mayor was right. Jake had sacrificed himself for the good of the town.

And yet he didn't look as if he was the least bit bothered by that fact. That heartwarming half smile lingered on his face as his eyes momentarily caught hers.

"Mr. Mayor, if you don't mind, I have one thing left to say," Jake said, his grin widening as his gaze swept the room.

"Please." The mayor gestured for him to

keep the floor. "You're more than welcome to continue."

"Avery Winslow," Jake said, his soft Texas accent as warm and rich as honey.

Avery started at the sound of her own name.

"Avery Winslow," he said again, "showed me and my family all about what living in a small town really means. She and her siblings opened their arms to us when they didn't have to." He stopped as a slight chuckled emerged from his lips. "She really, *really* didn't have to. And she had good reason to want nothing to do with me and mine, and she could easily have rejected us. Marston wanted to build right over the Meyers' cabin, which, as many of you know, she wanted—*wants*—to turn into a bed-and-breakfast to assist the guests who are visiting A New Leash on Love to get a service dog."

He gestured at Sissy. "As you may have heard, my own family has benefited greatly from this service, so I know more than anyone just how important Avery's goals are. The service dogs help so many people in so many ways. And though building a bed-and-breakfast is a longtime dream of hers, when all is said and done, her sweet, tender heart beats for the good of others."

He placed his palm over his heart and turned to Avery.

"And my heart," he continued, "beats for Avery."

Avery stood but felt as if she couldn't move a muscle. Their eyes met, and she saw something glowing in his gaze she'd never seen before.

Could it be?

"Lisa Gibbons?" Jake called, and Avery's best friend rushed forward, a pile of papers and folders in her arms.

"Lisa has been so kind as to help me jump through the hoops of paperwork necessary to work out how Avery can purchase the Meyers' cabin. I had no idea buying a house was so complicated."

Lisa giggled and threw her arms around Avery for a quick hug. Avery was so stunned at what was happening she still couldn't move or speak.

"But we have worked it out," Jake continued, his tone sending waves of warmth and happiness through her. "The cabin has passed inspection, and it's time to close on your dream house, Avery. You have a bed-and-breakfast in your future. Just sign on the dotted line, and it's all yours."

"Jake," she managed to choke out as tears burned in her eyes. "I— How did you—"

"With a lot of help from your friends and neighbors," Jake replied. "And I think you'll discover when it comes to remodeling the cabin to suit your specific needs, you'll find all the carpenters, plumbers and electricians you need, all willing to donate their services to the new bed-and-breakfast for A New Leash on Love."

Avery was seriously crying now, over-whelmed not only by Jake's goodness in orga-nizing this, but by all the people in this room right now, those who not only spoke love on Sunday mornings in church but showed it by the way they lived their lives.

She was blessed in so many ways.

And there stood Jake with his heartwarm-ing half smile, drinking it all in and enjoying every moment of Avery's surprise.

But what about him?

Had he given any thought to his own plans now that he was no longer working for Marston?

He'd go find another position, she supposed. A man with his talent, skills and natural charm should be able to get any job he wanted, anywhere he wanted.

And just like that, her moment of happiness was gone. Because she didn't want him and his precious family to go away.

Could she convince him to stay?

Jake had carefully planned every aspect of this evening, and so far it had gone off without a hitch. He'd been in cahoots with many of the helpful townspeople, and they'd all kept his little—okay, *big*—secret.

He'd really won the day when he'd pulled the rug out from under Marston Enterprises. He'd thought at the time it would stress him out, losing his job and his way to provide for his family.

But it hadn't. If anything, it felt as if a heavy weight had been lifted from his shoulders as he realized that, for some time now, he'd known what he was doing just wasn't right. Finally, he'd had the courage to stand up and say so.

He'd approached Lisa to find out about purchasing the Meyers' cabin. At first he'd thought to do it with his own money as a present to Avery, but Lisa had talked him out of that idea right quick. This was Avery's dream, and she'd been working toward it all her life. It should be hers to claim.

And now she could.

Avery stared in confusion at the pile of legal papers Lisa had tossed onto the table, and then she looked from Lisa to Jake, her eyes wide.

"What is this?" she queried again, either not understanding or more likely refusing to believe what was right in front of her eyes was true.

"Your dream come true, sweetie," Lisa offered. "Thanks to your man Jake here, all you have to do is sign, and we'll close on the cabin first thing tomorrow morning."

*Your man Jake.*

Wow, that sounded good.

And that's what he wanted most of all.

"So, sign already," he said, his voice rough with emotion. He cleared his throat and pulled a pen from the inside pocket of his suit jacket, handing it to her with a flourish.

Avery met his eyes, and their gazes held for a long moment before she took the pen from him and scribbled her name multiple times where Lisa indicated.

Jake stood back and let her have her moment, knowing the tears in her eyes were happy tears.

"I—I—" she stammered when Lisa announced the cabin was really and truly hers. She turned to the crowd. "Thank you. Thank you all for everything. Not just for the cabin, but for allowing me and my siblings to train our dogs around town. You all mean everything to me, and I'll never forget what you've done for me tonight."

The applause was deafening, and it warmed Jake's heart until he thought it might burst from pride. This woman deserved all this and more, and he hoped that by God's good pleasure, he could be the one to help give it to her.

He'd made it through Marston's presentation, even with his former Marston comrades glaring daggers at him. They had never been friends, anyway—not like the ones he'd made in Whispering Pines. He'd been able to stay focused for when it was his turn to tell the truth and expose Marston for what it was.

He'd watched in the background as Avery

was given her dream cabin, ready to build her bed-and-breakfast.

More than anything, he longed to be at her side for that.

To be at her side for always.

As the applause started to die away, Jake pulled a velvet ring box from the inner pocket of his suit jacket and knelt just behind the woman he loved.

"Avery," he said, his throat closing around the word.

When she turned, she didn't immediately see him kneeling in front of her, a ring box open to display a large diamond solitaire surrounded by smaller stones that set off the larger diamond perfectly.

Then she looked down, met his gaze and cried out in surprise.

"Oh!"

Her hands went to her face, covering her expression so he couldn't tell what she was thinking.

It was too late for him to back out now, after coming this far.

"Avery," he said again. "I—don't have a job."

What a stupid thing to say. He was completely blowing this.

"What I mean to say is that—that is, I want to—"

"Yes," she exclaimed, holding out her left hand to him. Her face was glowing, and the love in her eyes was shining through to him in a way even words could not. "Absolutely yes, yes, yes!"

Jake felt as if someone had let all the air out of his body. Every muscle relaxed as he slid the ring onto her finger.

The crowd was cheering so loud he could barely hear himself think, which he supposed was okay, since he was having trouble putting together a single thought, anyway.

"Stand up, you," Avery said, pulling him to his feet.

He stood and held her hand up, admiring the way the diamond sparkled in the light. He kissed the spot where the diamond sat. Then Lottie ran to him and launched herself into his arms.

"Hey, Lottie, what do you think of this ring?" he asked.

"Sparkly!"

"It sure is beautiful, isn't it?" Avery agreed.

"Do you know what it means that Daddy gave me this ring?"

"He wants to marry you and make you part of our family," she announced, almost as if she was reading a definition out of a dictionary. "Except he didn't."

"Didn't what, sweetie?" Jake's mom asked, joining them in the middle of the aisle.

"Daddy didn't ask Miss Avery to marry him. He needs to watch some of my cartoons so he can see how to do it like the princes do."

Jake's face heated. He'd had every word and motion planned out in advance, but the second he'd dropped to one knee he'd become a blithering idiot. He'd blown the whole thing so badly even his three-year-old daughter had noticed.

And of course he'd decided to propose in front of the whole town.

*Way to go, Cutter.*

Avery chuckled. "Those princes do have a one up on the rest of us, don't they? But that's okay. I understood what your daddy was trying to say, even if he didn't say the words. I can't think of anything I'd like more than to become part of your family. But first I want to know what you think about it, Lottie. It's important to me that you want me to be part of your family, too."

"I get to keep Sissy, right?" she asked.

"Of course. She's a member of your—uh—*our* family, too."

Jake grinned so hard he thought his face might split, and that was nothing to say of the way his heart welled in his chest.

*Our family.*

She couldn't have said anything in the world that sounded better to him.

"Avery, honey," he said, drawing her attention back to him and framing her face with one hand.

She looked up at him with so much love in her eyes, he counted himself the most blessed man in the world. And he wanted to tell her so.

He ran his thumb across her cheek as he spoke. "I messed this up big-time. I had it all planned out what I was gonna say, all these big declarations about my feelings and how I can't live without you, and then my tongue got all twisted in knots, and I forgot everything. I love you, Avery. I think I have for a while now, although it's taken some time to get into this thick skull of mine. You've changed my life, sweetheart, and all for the better. I want to share everything with you. My heart. My family."

"Our home?" Avery said with a knowing smile.

*Our* home.

The words melted his heart like butter.

But he hadn't gotten that far yet. He hadn't even been sure she would agree to be his wife, after all was said and done. He had figured he ought not to make any other permanent plans until that part of his life was sewn up.

He supposed they'd have to look for a house of their own. He and his mother were only renting the small cabin by the river, and Avery lived with all her siblings. He'd have to get his mom set up in an apartment. As for him, Avery and Lottie—

"The bed-and-breakfast," Avery prompted. "It has a mother-in-law suite that will be perfect for whoever runs the place on a day-by-day basis. Word has it that you're out of a job now, and a little birdie told me you had a bit of training in culinary arts and you're a pretty good cook."

"I have to admit, that industrial kitchen of

yours scratches an itch of mine to make monkey pancakes."

"Kitchen of *ours*," she corrected.

"Daddy makes really good chocolate-chip monkey pancakes," Lottie said, smacking her lips.

"Or blueberry, if you prefer," he tempted.

"Sounds good to me," she said. "But do you know what I'd rather have right now, even more than blueberry monkey pancakes?

"This."

Her eyes sparkled as she pulled his face down to hers and pressed her lips to his.

When Avery had come to the council meeting this evening, she could never in a million years have envisioned the way it would have turned out.

She'd thought she was going to leave the council meeting tonight entirely defeated. Instead, she was walking on air. It was truly a dream, a happily-ever-after beyond what she could ever have imagined.

Jake handed Lottie off to his mother and framed both sides of her face, kissing her thoroughly and leaving her no doubt that this was real and not a dream. His lips were soft, and when she placed her palm against his chest she could feel the rapid beating of his heart that matched her own.

She had a fiancé, and as soon as they were married, she would waste no time in adopting Lottie as her own daughter. No more worries about being doubly heartbroken.

Now she was doubly blessed. Triply blessed, actually, with a wonderful mother-in-law in Elaine.

Jake had put a ring on it to make certain she knew he meant forever.

It was only after several minutes that she realized they weren't alone. She'd been so caught up in the moment and focused on what was happening between her and Jake that all the cheers and applause had swept right past her unheard.

But the whole town was there, and now their friends and neighbors were pressing in on them to wish them well. Everyone was hugging her and shaking hands with Jake, excited not only for the way things had turned out with the retreat of the Marston resort but most especially the romantic gesture at the end that would keep Jake and his family in town permanently.

Jake let out a Texas whoop that reminded

Avery of the very first time they'd met, when he'd unfolded himself from that silly red Mustang and hollered in delight for no apparent reason at all. She was going to have to have a talk with him about that Mustang, because she was not going to put any future children of theirs into that car for any reason.

Future children.

How wonderful that sounded. How right and perfect it was for the two of them to join their hearts and lives. She was more than ready and willing to welcome Lottie as her daughter, as well. She already loved the little girl.

After a good half hour of congratulations and well wishes, the hall started clearing out, and Avery finally made it back to Jake's side. He was holding a sleeping Lottie, whose head rested across his broad shoulder.

"I can't believe you planned all this for me. The presentation against Marston was amazing. Getting with Lisa to work out the details of our bed-and-breakfast was incredible. And most of all—" her throat closed up as she fought to find the words that would express the feelings in her heart "—that you would propose to me in front of everyone.

There are no words to express how special that is to me."

"Yeah, well, it would have helped if I'd memorized my lines a little better, don't you think? I don't know, honey—like, *Will you marry me?*"

"My answer would have been the same no matter how you phrased it," she assured him. "Or even if you hadn't said anything at all. This beautiful ring gave me a pretty good notion of your intentions."

He chuckled. "Yeah. I guess it would."

"And as it was, I never got to tell you what's in *my* heart."

He wrapped his free arm around her shoulder and led her toward the door. "And that would be what?" he asked in his warm Texas drawl.

"That I love you. More than I ever could have thought it was possible to love someone. You drove me absolutely crazy when we first met, and yet somehow you wiggled your way into my heart."

"It's my inherent charm," he said with a toothy grin. "All the ladies love it, but you're the only woman I want."

She rolled her eyes and slapped his bicep.

"Of course you would think you're God's gift. One thing you're not short on is confidence. Or swagger."

"Now, the swagger comes naturally, darlin'," he assured her. "But confidence? I was sweating bullets tonight thinking you might reject me."

"Then, why on earth did you propose in public? Wouldn't it have made more sense to do it when it was just the two of us alone together?"

"Because I want everyone in Whispering Pines to know just how much I love you, Avery. My love doesn't depend on whether you'd said yes or no—although I much prefer the way things turned out, so don't get me wrong there. But if I could, I'd crow it from the mountaintops."

He flapped his arm like a chicken. "I love Avery Winslow!" he called out.

"Shh!" Avery whispered. "You'll wake up Lottie."

He chuckled and kissed the top of his daughter's curly-haired head. "She was over the moon when I told her I was going to ask you to be my wife."

"She couldn't possibly be as happy as I am

right now." Avery leaned her cheek against Jake's strong arm. "So much has happened tonight, my head is spinning."

"I'm just glad I have a job. That has to be a new record. Getting fired and hired in the same evening. You're right about a lot happening tonight. And I'm looking forward to the future, when I can add a second ring to that first one and make you my wife in truth."

He kissed her forehead, and her heart flipped over. "Please tell me you don't want to wait long before we have our wedding," he pleaded, offering her a pathetic look.

"As far as I'm concerned, the less planning we have to do, the better. We're going to have enough organizing to do on our new bed-and-breakfast."

"I say we just do a small ceremony with family. Soon. You think?" he suggested, then seemed to be holding his breath for her answer.

"As far as I'm concerned, it can't come soon enough," she agreed, wrapping herself into his arms for another long kiss.

# *Epilogue*

## *One Year Later*

Jake whistled as he flipped the pancakes on the griddle and turned back to whipping up a big batch of scrambled eggs. His mother was over for a visit and was already seated at the kitchen table the family used for their meals.

Jake was making breakfast for everyone. Like Lottie, breakfast was his mother's favorite meal of the day, and it was likewise his favorite to cook.

They were between guests for the service-dog program and intended to spend the weekend hanging out as a family. Fresh snow had fallen, and Jake thought they might all go out and build a snowman, and maybe have a snowball fight. Avery loved to play. Snowball fights were right up her alley.

Their wedding had been beautiful—or rather, Avery had been beautiful walking down the aisle. He didn't remember much else, except hopefully that he'd gotten all the words right this time.

Now it was everyday life he thoroughly enjoyed. Weddings were a onetime event. Marriages were a lifetime of daily love and laughter.

He valued living in a small mountain town more than he could ever have imagined back when he lived in the city. Lottie was going to preschool now and had made lots of friends. Avery still did the books for the family businesses while he did the day-to-day running of the bed-and-breakfast—all of the cooking and interacting with the guests, signing them in and out and making sure they knew how to get around town.

Every morning, he and Avery would spend time together, just the two of them. First they'd strip all the beds and start the laundry, then make all the beds up new again as they spoke about their plans for the day. And then at night they'd often gather with their guests around the community fireplace at the center of the cabin.

This was truly the life he'd never even known he wanted, and he couldn't imagine being any happier than he was at this moment.

"Breakfast is on," he called down the hallway to the suite they'd recently renovated for their family. "Who wants monkey pancakes? I've got chocolate chip or blueberry just waiting for you over here."

Lottie dashed into the kitchen, Sissy right at her heel. She was still experiencing epileptic seizures, but the local doctor had her on a new medicine that seemed to be helping with both the frequency and intensity of them. Most of all, though, Sissy had made an enormous difference in Lottie's life, always there to protect and watch over Jake's little girl.

Avery yawned as she followed Lottie into the kitchen, pulling her shoulder-length blond hair back into a ponytail and fastening it with a clip. She was still in her pajamas, which she'd covered with a robe. Her pink slippers were peeking out from underneath.

That wasn't like her. She was usually a

morning person, an early riser with a fountain full of energy.

"Sorry," she murmured, rubbing the sleep from her eyes. "I'm just so tired lately."

Jake flashed her a worried frown, wondering if something might be wrong with her, but she gestured him away, sliding into the seat beside Lottie.

"Monkey pancakes?" she asked the little girl, who, as usual, answered with a happy squeal.

"Daddy knows all our favorites, doesn't he?" Avery asked, and then said, "Thank you, Daddy."

Lottie added another excited squeak.

Jake wondered if she was ever going to grow out of that phase, or whether Lottie would continue to punctuate her excitement in such an earsplitting way for the rest of her life—or at least her childhood.

Squeals and squeaks were the sounds of a happy house, he supposed.

Jake placed monkey pancakes in front of Lottie, and Avery scooped some eggs onto the little girl's plate and doused Mr. Monkey with some real maple syrup.

"Yum. I'm absolutely famished," said

Avery as Jake placed her plate in front of her, her pancakes also in the shape of a monkey. "I hope you made extra for me, because I can't seem to get enough of them."

When they'd all been served, Jake sat at the head of the table, and they all joined hands to thank the Lord for all their blessings. And he had plenty. He took a moment longer today, just looking around at each family member as gratitude filled his heart for each one.

After they'd eaten, Avery said, "You know, I was out shopping the other day when I found what I believe may be the perfect T-shirt for Lottie."

Jake raised his eyebrows. Okay, fine, so Avery had gone shopping. But this seemed like an odd time to mention it.

"Hold on just a second, and I'll be right back with it. I can't wait to show you."

Jake and his mother exchanged glances as Avery raced out of the room and back into their bedroom. Moments later, she reappeared, her face full of color—more color than she should have had, given the short distance she'd had to walk. Jake once again wondered if maybe she was coming down with the flu or something.

"What's your favorite color, Lottie?" she asked, although Jake knew Avery was already aware of the answer.

"Purple," Lottie declared.

"I thought so. And that's why when I saw this purple shirt, I knew it would be perfect for you."

Avery held up the shirt, but she accidentally held it backward.

"It's wrong way around, honey," Jake told her. "I'm assuming there's sparkles or something on the front?"

Avery laughed. "Or something."

Then, her smile widening, she turned the T-shirt around so everyone could see what was on the front.

In big, sparkly letters, it declared:

*I'm the Big Sister.*

Jake gave a good Texas whoop, and his mother exclaimed in delight. Lottie just looked from one to the other, confused.

Jake jumped up and ran around to envelop his wife in his arms, picking her up and swinging her around with another big whoop. Then he realized the import of what he was doing and gently set her down. He had to treat her with extra care.

Avery chuckled and shook her head as if she could hear his thoughts. "You won't break me—or the baby—by giving me a hug," she assured him.

*The baby.*

She took his large hand and placed it over her abdomen.

"The doctor says I'm eight weeks along," she informed him with a gentle smile. "I won't start showing for a while, but the next time we go in to see the doctor we'll be able to hear the baby's heartbeat."

Avery slid into the chair next to Lottie and helped her to put on her new shirt, then read the words aloud to her.

"Do you know what that means, Lottie?" Jake asked gently. "Do you understand what's going on?"

Lottie wrinkled her nose and paused in concentration.

"You're going to be a big sister, sweetheart," Jake's mom explained.

"That's right, Lottie. You're going to have a baby brother or sister in—" Jake's heart was hammering wildly as he glanced up at Avery for the answer.

"October," she suppled.

As Jake pulled Avery into his arms and swung her around, kissing her over and over, Lottie gave her very first Texas—or maybe it was really a Colorado—whoop.

Just like her daddy.

* * * * *

*If you loved this story,*
*pick up the previous book*
*in the Rocky Mountain Family series*
*from bestselling author Deb Kastner,*
The Black Sheep's Salvation,
*and be sure to check out*
*some of Deb's previous books:*

The Cowboy's Twins
Mistletoe Daddy
The Cowboy's Baby Blessing
And Cowboy Makes Three
A Christmas Baby for the Cowboy
Her Forgotten Cowboy

*Available now from Love Inspired!*

*Find more great reads at*
*www.LoveInspired.com*

Dear Reader,

I know this book is coming out in January 2021, but as I'm writing this, I'm currently quarantined at home here in Colorado because of the COVID-19 virus, something that will definitely go down in the history books. The governor issued a stay-at-home order, and we are all doing our part by not leaving our homes any more than necessary.

By the time you're reading this, I hope the virus is a thing of the past, but it has really made me consider just how important inspirational romances are to my readers. The one thing I can offer is a Happily-Ever-After in God's grace, and that I am grateful to do as I sit down to my computer to write every day.

Please, hug your loved ones. You never know what tomorrow will bring. I wish you all every blessing.

I'm always delighted to hear from you, dear readers, and I love to connect socially. To get regular updates, please sign up for my newsletter at http://www.debkastnerbooks.

com. Come join me on Facebook at http://www.Facebook.com/debkastnerbooks, and you can catch me on Twitter @debkastner.

Dare to Dream,

Deb Kastner

# THE 2020 LOVE INSPIRED CHRISTMAS COLLECTION

## Buy 3 and get 1 FREE!

This collection is guaranteed to provide you with many hours of cozy reading pleasure with uplifting romances that celebrate the joy of love at Christmas.

---

**YES!** Please send me **The 2020 Love Inspired Christmas Collection** in Larger Print. This collection begins with ONE FREE book and 2 FREE gifts (approx. retail value of the gifts is $7.99 each) in the first shipment. Along with my FREE book, I'll get another 3 Larger Print books! If I do not cancel, I will continue to receive four books a month for four more months. I'll pay just $20.97 U.S./$23.97 CAN., plus $1.99 U.S./$4.99 CAN. for shipping and handling per shipment.* I understand that accepting the free books and gifts places me under no obligation to buy anything. I can always return a shipment and cancel at any time. My free books and gifts are mine to keep no matter what I decide.

☐ 299 HCN 5494          ☐ 499 HCN 5494

Name (please print)

Address                                                                                    Apt. #

City                              State/Province                         Zip/Postal Code

### Mail to the Harlequin Reader Service:
**IN U.S.A.:** P.O. Box 1341, Buffalo, NY. 14240-8531
**IN CANADA:** P.O. Box 603, Fort Erie, Ontario L2A 5X3

---